"Do you really think that? Or is this just flattery?"

"It's the truth. Yeah, I'll admit I feel like a teenaged boy who got pulled onstage with his favorite singer right now." *Damn. Didn't mean to say that aloud.* He ran a hand over his face. "But I meant every word I said."

The soft smile on her face grew even bigger. "Wow."

He smiled back, still trying to read that look in her eyes. *What is she thinking right now?*

A moment later, she leaned toward him. Her small hand came up to cup his jaw. "You're quite the charmer, Campbell Monroe."

"Not really." He couldn't tear his eyes away from hers. His face tingled beneath the warmth of her touch. "I'm just honest."

She tilted her head, letting her eyes drift closed as her lips formed that unmistakable pucker shape.

He didn't know how they'd gotten here but he wasn't about to turn down an invitation like that. He placed a hand on her shoulder, then gently touched his lips to hers.

Dear Reader,

Thanks for picking up a copy of *Love for All Time*.
I hope you enjoy returning to Sapphire Shores
with me. Lots of things are changing on the island,
and the characters are undergoing changes, as well.
Campbell Monroe has thought himself impervious to
developing feelings for a woman. Now Sierra Dandridge
is going to challenge everything he thought he knew.
I hope you enjoy the story, and I look forward to your
feedback on social media or via my website contact form.

Best,

Kianna

LOVE
FOR *All* TIME

KIANNA ALEXANDER

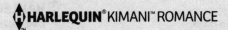
HARLEQUIN® KIMANI™ ROMANCE

41938

Recycling programs
for this product may
not exist in your area.

ISBN-13: 978-1-335-21683-0

Love for All Time

Copyright © 2018 by Eboni Manning

For questions and comments about the quality of this book please contact us at CustomerService@Harlequin.com.

HARLEQUIN®

Printed in U.S.A.

www.Harlequin.com

Kianna Alexander, like any good Southern belle, wears many hats: loving wife, doting mama, advice-dispensing sister and gabbing girlfriend. She's a voracious reader, an amateur seamstress and occasional painter in oils. Chocolate, American history, sweet tea and Idris Elba are a few of her favorite things. A native of the Tar Heel state, Kianna still lives there with her husband, two kids and a collection of well-loved vintage '80s Barbie dolls. You can keep up with Kianna's releases and appearances by signing up for her mailing list at www.authorkiannaalexander.com/sign-up.

Books by Kianna Alexander

Harlequin Kimani Romance

This Tender Melody
Every Beat of My Heart
A Sultry Love Song
Tempo of Love
A Love Like This
A San Diego Romance
Love for All Time

Visit the Author Page at Harlequin.com for more titles.

For my brother Eric.
May you discover the purpose that lies within you,
and may your dreams become reality.

Chapter 1

"Do we have to film this scene today?" Sitting in the back of the chauffeur-driven sedan, Sierra Dandridge looked hopefully toward the passenger seat.

Up front, Jazmin shook her head. "I don't even know why you asked me that, girl." Having often said she didn't like being chauffeured around, she always sat up front.

Sierra sighed at the inevitable response. *Me, either.* "It was worth a shot."

Jazmin chuckled. "No, it wasn't." She turned around to look her way. "You know I sympathize with you, as a friend. But as a producer of the show, I'm gonna need you to get it together."

Rolling her eyes, Sierra flopped against the

leather seat. "I know, I know." It wasn't as if she disliked her role on the new drama series *The Shores*. Even though the show had cast her to play "to type," and she hated being pigeonholed, she still enjoyed the role. As filming locations went, though, the island of Sapphire Shores was about as dull as it could get. "I guess we may as well get it over with."

"Don't worry. This is your last scene with Mia for at least a few days or so."

"I'll take whatever break from her you can give me."

"I know you and Mia aren't exactly close," Jazmin quipped. "But she's your colleague. I expect you two to keep it professional."

Rolling her eyes at the mention of that name, Sierra nodded. "Always. I never mess around when it comes to my coins. But I can't speak for Mia."

Mia Leigh, the lead actress on *The Shores*, had become the bane of her existence. This season's script had Sierra and Mia cast as "frenemies," complete with the much younger Mia being slick at the mouth with Sierra. That would be fine with Sierra, if only Mia could keep that drama on the set. Petty as she was, Ms. Leigh seemed to have a real-life vendetta against Sierra.

"If she wants to keep this job, she'll get her attitude together," Jazmin declared. "Casting isn't my department, but I won't hesitate to go to the higher-ups if Mia insists on being the problem child."

Sierra reached into her bag, taking out her compact. She looked at her reflection, making sure the makeup artist's work remained intact. After running a brush through her hair and tucking it and the compact away, she turned her attention back to the passing scenery.

Despite the island's total lack of nightlife or entertainment, it was one of the most beautiful places she'd ever worked, in terms of scenery. The day was a bit overcast, but sunlight peeked through the clouds to sparkle on the crystal surface of the Atlantic. The picturesque scene reminded her of when she'd filmed *High Treason* off the coast of Maine. She hoped the nice weather would hold, at least until she got back to her hotel. It was a mid-September Monday, and in the few weeks she'd been on the island, she'd noticed how quickly the weather seemed to change.

The car slowed to go over a series of speed bumps leading into the Tracemore Plaza area. As the vehicle rounded the traffic circle and moved toward an empty space in the parking lot, she could see other members of the show's cast and crew gathered outside the entrance to Della's Deli. The sandwich shop, one of their most used filming locations, served great food and had a lovely atmosphere. *Although Mia's attitude ruins it every time.* She rolled her eyes.

The driver parked the car and walked around to open Sierra's door. Jazmin, ever the girl-next-door, saw herself out of the passenger seat as the driver opened the back door and helped Sierra to her feet.

Slinging her purse over her shoulder, she drew in a deep breath of the salty air.

She followed Jazmin toward the entrance to the deli. As her friend donned her headset and began conversing with the crew, Sierra cut through the gaggle of people, waving and acknowledging many of them, but choosing not to engage Mia. Once she made her way through, she waited by the glass doors for her cue. Leaning against the exterior wall, she contented herself with watching the camerawoman, boom operator and lighting tech ready their equipment for the scene they were about to film. Watching the cast and crew buzzing around, preparing to shoot a scene, always filled her with a sense of anticipation. She loved what she did, loved bringing each character she portrayed to life in her own special way. Each scene she filmed gave her a new opportunity to do what she loved most. A smile touched her lips.

The smile quickly faded as she noticed Mia strutting her way. She couldn't ever remember having seen Mia just…walk. She always strutted, much like a peacock with its colors on full display. Tall and lithe, the fair-skinned, dark-eyed twentysomething was runway beautiful. That made sense; she'd parlayed her background in modeling high fashion into an acting career. She was dressed to the nines, though some of the credit for that went to the wardrobe department. Her bright red handbag stood out in contrast to her muted royal blue romper. Her close-cropped black hair, sprayed and coiffed to perfection, barely moved as she approached.

Mia's lips spread into a plastic smile that showed most of her teeth. "Hey, Sierra."

"Hello, Mia." She'd spoken to her, and hoped that would be the end of their interaction.

To her chagrin, Mia continued. "So, are you ready for this scene? The script says we're supposed to be arguing today."

What kind of silly question is that? What, does she think I just roll up to the set without reading the damn script? Gathering her patience, she nodded. "I know, and yes, I'm ready."

"Arguing with you isn't that hard for me." She looked off to the side in a dramatic fashion. "Since I don't really like you that much."

She sighed. "And why is that, Mia?"

Mia's wayward gaze returned to Sierra's face. "You're a fading flower that refuses to acknowledge the new blossoms in the garden." She reached up to adjust a tendril of hair by her ear.

Sierra tipped her head to one side, offering a cold smile that didn't reach her eyes. "Mia, you're an intelligent girl. You even turn a decent metaphor. But there are a lot of things about this industry that you just don't know."

Folding her arms over her chest, Mia snapped, "So what? I'm young, I've got talent and determination, and that's all I need."

"If only that were true." Sierra had been in the

game long enough to know the kinds of pitfalls that awaited budding actresses. *She's going to need more than her looks and her stubbornness if she really wants to make it.* In any other case, she'd be reaching out to mentor a young actress just starting out in the business. But it was clear Mia was more interested in being catty than in learning from someone more experienced.

Jazmin walked over then. Taking a moment to look from one to the other, she paused, then stood between them. Her expression said she sensed the tension hanging in the air. "Everything okay over here, ladies? We're getting ready to start the filming."

Sierra nodded tightly, because she was eager to get through the scene and away from the "fatal blossom."

"Oh, everything's fine between us," Mia trilled. "My mother taught me to always respect my *elders*." On the heels of her declaration, she turned and strutted away.

A deep sigh left Sierra's lips.

Jazmin touched her shoulder. "Remember your promise, Sierra."

"Don't worry, I haven't forgotten. I'm going to keep it professional, whether she does or not." Like she'd said before, Sierra never messed around when it came to her money. She loved her role on the show, and she intended to keep this job going for as long as she could.

And in spite of Mia's funky attitude, she wasn't

about to let a naive, cocky little upstart interfere with her earning potential.

Drawing a deep breath, she went to take her mark for the start of the scene. It called for her to be standing next to Mia, near the door of the deli. Ignoring Mia's smug expression, she waited.

When the cameras and lights turned her way, she came alive.

With a cup of coffee in hand, Campbell Monroe reclined against the cushioned backrest of the bench. He was sitting in a booth at Della's, enjoying a late lunch. It had been past two when he'd finally left the office and made the quick drive to the restaurant. Now, as the three o'clock hour neared, he was capping off his lunch with a cup of coffee and a slice of Della's famous apple crumb cake.

He figured the late lunch would make the perfect segue into his next meeting. A client had requested to meet him here, to discuss the possibility of purchasing a condominium. He'd told the woman it would take some work to secure a unit, and he'd meant it. Since Devon Franklin had opened his newly built studio about two months ago, and started filming his show *The Shores* almost immediately after, Sapphire Shores had seen a large influx in population. The show's talent, crew and studio employees had moved onto the island, mixing with the already robust crowd of tourists, to create a perfect storm of growth. Since Monroe Holdings, Incorporated, the real estate empire started by Campbell's parents, owned most of the properties on the island, business was brisker than ever.

He pushed away the ceramic plate, which now held only crumbs as evidence of the cake he'd devoured. One of Della's staff members dutifully whisked the plate away, just as he saw the lady he was to meet with entering. She was older than him, in her mid- to upper fifties, he guessed, and she moved with an air of certainty and grace.

Campbell stood as she approached the booth, extending his hand to her. "Mrs. Fairbanks. Lovely to see you."

She nodded, shook his head. "Nice to meet you, Mr. Monroe."

He gestured to the bench across the table from him. "Please, have a seat. Let's talk about what you're looking for."

She nodded and slipped into the seat.

He sat once she was settled. "Would you like anything before we get started? A beverage? Maybe some of Della's apple crumb cake?"

She shook her head. "No, thanks." Pushing her gold, wire-rimmed glasses up on the bridge of her nose, she fixed her gaze on him. "I'm looking for a nice, low-maintenance place I can use as a vacation retreat during the colder months. Winters are brutal up in Philadelphia, and I'd love to have a place I can escape to before the snow hits."

"Sounds reasonable. We've had an influx of folks

coming onto the island recently, so you'll need a healthy budget in order to secure a unit at this point." He scratched his chin, waiting. He'd been property manager at MHI for over a decade now, and he never used a hard sell. He simply listened to his clients and tried to meet their needs.

She quoted a number. "Will that be enough?"

He smiled. "Certainly. I have just the place in mind for you." With her generous budget, she'd have her pick of some of the choicest units in Cape Glenn or Shoreside Manor, the two most upscale developments on the island. "You'll have a lot of flexibility with that."

"Great. I figured units would be hard to come by, what with the show filming here and all that."

His brow hitched. "So, you know about *The Shores*?"

She nodded, her expression brightening. "Sure do. I love that show." She looked wistful for a moment. "My late husband was always on me about watching the soaps, but I never did give them up. I love a messy plot."

He chuckled, shaking his head. "From what I heard, messy plot is at the heart of the show."

"You don't watch it?"

"No. Can't say I have much free time these days." Since his little sister, Hadley, had married actor-turned-producer-and-studio-head Devon Franklin, she'd been pulling a lot fewer hours at the office. That meant that the pile of work he often left for her went unfinished, unless he did it himself. Her absence had forced him to take on more of the work-load than he was accustomed to.

"To be honest—" she lowered her voice to a whisper "—that's why I wanted to meet you at Della's. It says on the website that the show films here sometimes, and I'm hoping to catch a bit of the action while I'm here."

Amused, he nodded. "Who knows? Maybe you'll luck out." He'd seen the headlines in the local paper, and the reviews comparing the show to the old night-time soaps like *Knot's Landing*. While his mother had been a fan of those shows, he didn't really re-member much about them. So far, the only compel-ling reason he saw to watch was Sierra.

"I hope so." His client glanced around, then pointed to the wall mural depicting an undersea scene. "I recognize that wall. I've seen it on the show."

He thought it better to steer the conversation back to her search for property. "So, how long will you be in town?"

"About another week. I'm staying with my son and his wife over in Wilmington."

"Great. Then we'll need to schedule a time that's good for you to tour a few units, and…"

He stopped midsentence as a menagerie of cam-eras, flashing lights and bodies burst through the door into the deli's interior. Knowing right away what was up, he shook his head. *Looks like Mrs. Fairbanks is getting her wish.*

Mrs. Fairbanks whirled around, then stood. "Goodness. It's happening."

The gaggle of bodies by the door parted long enough for two women to make their way through to the counter. The cameras were trained on them, recording their every step.

Campbell watched them, too. The tall, youthful one with the red purse was attractive, and looked somewhat familiar. He knew some of the cast, just from interacting with them. The island wasn't terribly large, so he'd met a number of them. *That's, uh, what was her name? Megan? Martha?*

He shifted his focus to the more petite woman. Sierra Dandridge, the famed actress, didn't require an introduction. The newest, and possibly the most famous cast member of *The Shores*, she'd only recently arrived on the island. A formfitting black dress with long sleeves hugged her shapely, compact frame, and she stood confidently on a pair of tall, impossibly narrow black stilettos. She wore her hair in long waves down her back, and it was currently dyed a silvery lavender. The color of her hair, along with her closed-off stance, perfectly fit the "Ice Queen" image the press ascribed to her. Still, Campbell couldn't remember the last time he'd seen anyone so strikingly beautiful. He'd had a crush on her since he'd seen her in the spy thriller *Waltz at Midnight* several years ago. It amazed him that she was just as gorgeous in person as she was on screen.

Mrs. Fairbanks, vibrating with excitement, stared

in the direction of the cast and crew. "I'm not going to go over there. I know better than to interrupt the filming. But this is so exciting!"

Campbell chuckled. He'd managed to avoid the filming for most of the three months it had been going on. But his turn to be a part of the madness had apparently come around.

Once he got Mrs. Fairbanks to sit back down, he scheduled an appointment with her for later in the week. By then, Sierra and her costar were in a booth on the far side of the room, with the show's crew clustered around them to capture their conversation. That freed up the front entrance, making a much appreciated path of escape.

He stood, extending his hand toward Mrs. Fairbanks. "It was lovely talking to you, and I look forward to our meeting."

"Thank you, Mr. Monroe." She barely took her eyes off the hubbub near the booth. "Are you really rushing off? Don't you want to watch the filming?"

He shook his head. "Nah. I'm not really into that sort of thing. Besides, I have a ton of work waiting on my desk."

"Okay, then. Have a good day. I'm gonna stay, and see if I can get some autographs when they finish!" The giddiness came through in her voice.

"Best of luck." With a chuckle, Campbell turned and walked away. With a parting wave to Della and her staff, he swung open the door and stepped out into the humid afternoon air.

As he climbed into his black-on-black convertible, his mind strayed again to his beautiful celebrity crush, currently sitting less than fifty yards away from him.

With a wry smile, he dropped the top and started the engine.

So close, and yet so far.

Chapter 2

Tuesday morning, Sierra's hand grasped the cool steel of the door handle at Monroe Holdings, Incorporated. Before she could pull it open, she noticed a tall, handsome brotha approaching from the other side. She stepped back as he pushed the door open.

She started to introduce herself. "Good morning, I'm…"

The man smiled, his teeth as brilliant and white as a polished string of pearls. "I know who you are. Good morning, Miss Dandridge. Welcome to MHI."

"Thank you." She entered the building and he closed the door behind her. They stood only a few feet apart, and with each inhaled breath, she took in a bit of his cologne. It smelled expensive, woodsy and masculine.

She looked him over. He towered over her by a good four inches. He had dark hair, trimmed close, and dark brown eyes flecked with gold. A thin, neatly trimmed goatee framed his full lips, and a small diamond stud sparkled in his right earlobe. His body, fit and athletic, made the perfect canvas to display his tailored royal blue suit, crisp white shirt and bright green tie.

She brought her gaze back up to his face, and she recalled seeing him in Della's the previous day. She could also feel his unveiled scrutiny as he stared at her. Realizing one of them had to speak so they wouldn't spend the morning staring at each other, she asked, "And you are..."

He seemed to snap out of it; chuckled. "Forgive me. I'm Campbell Monroe." He extended his hand to shake hers. "I'll be helping you choose a rental unit."

She returned his firm handshake. "Great. It's nice to meet you, Mr. Monroe."

Flashing that gorgeous smile again, he shook his head. "No need to be so formal, Ms. Dandridge. Call me Campbell, or Cam."

"Okay, Campbell." She smiled back, careful not to oversell it. Her pulse raced, but he didn't need to know that.

"Follow me." He started walking toward a corridor to the right.

She followed him until he led her into his office.

He sat behind the large oak desk and gestured for her to sit, as well. Taking the upholstered chair opposite him, she placed her purse on her lap. The space appeared just as masculine as its occupant. The walls, painted a deep shade of burgundy, hosted his bachelor's and master's degrees, several sports and movie posters, and a few modern art pieces. The tall shelves lining the walls were filled with various nonfiction titles, and a few trophies and knickknacks. When her eyes swung to the movie poster hanging on the wall directly behind his desk, she couldn't help smiling.

"So, Ms. Dandridge. We're excited to have an actress of your caliber staying with us here in Sapphire Shores."

His voice drew her attention and her gaze back to his handsome face. "Thank you, Campbell, that's very kind."

"I mean, *Waltz at Midnight* is one of my favorite movies of all time, mainly because of your stellar performance." He gestured to the movie poster behind him. "That's one of my most treasured possessions."

"I'm flattered. It was only my third film, but I really did enjoy playing the role." Her cheeks warmed a bit. She wasn't an egomaniac, but she'd thought she'd gotten past having a compliment affect her this way. In truth, it had been a minute since she'd been complimented by someone this fine. She sensed that he was very much a fan of her work, but she didn't want to use the whole appointment on conversation about her past roles.

As if he sensed her thoughts, he opened his desk drawer and pulled out two booklets. "While I'm a big fan of your work, I don't want to waste your time. So, let's talk about the kind of rental unit you'd like."

Grateful for the change of topic, she looked at the two glossy, full-color booklets he slid her way. "The Glenn and Shoreside Manor."

"Those are our most upscale developments on the island, and also our newest ones. The Glenn opened back in May, and Shoreside Manor in July." He rested his elbows on the desk and tented his fingers. "So, why don't you tell me the top three amenities that are most important to you."

She nodded. "I'd like a good deal of privacy, easy access to a gym or workout room, and security."

He scratched his chin. "Based on what you're saying, I'd recommend The Glenn. They're large luxury condominium units, and there's a lot less traffic and noise on the inlet side of the island."

She listened as he described square footage of the units, the laundry valet service and the well-appointed clubhouse, complete with workout room. One thing she'd requested, though, was left out of his description. "Everything you've mentioned sounds wonderful, Campbell. But what about the security?"

He snapped his fingers. "Yes, sorry about that. The Glenn is a gated community with twenty-four-hour surveillance, both remotely and through the on-site guard."

"I'm assuming the guard has a station at the entrance gate?"

"Yes."

"What about security for the individual units?"

His brow cocked as if the question surprised him, but he slid smoothly into an answer. "Each unit has an electronic security system. Cameras are placed all around the property, and every square inch has coverage."

She shifted in her seat. "That sounds great. But what if I require something more? Is it possible for me to get a security guard for my unit?"

He frowned a bit. "I'm not sure that would be necessary, Ms. Dandridge. You won't find a safer place in the country than our little island."

"That may be so, but this is a unique situation. In my line of work, I've seen what people are capable of. I've dealt with stalkers and crazed fans in the past, and I'd rather not do it again." She decided not to tell him about the guy she'd found scaling the fence at her house in Los Angeles, or the one who'd tried spying on her with a drone. At least not now.

Sitting back in his chair, he looked thoughtful for a moment. "I may be able to arrange something for you, but it will take some time. The Glenn isn't staffed for that sort of thing."

"I can understand that. I would really like a guard,

though, and I'd really appreciate it if you could make that happen." She returned the booklets to him.

"No problem." He picked up a pen from a cup on his desk. "Let me show you the video tour of the unit, so you can see how it's laid out." He entered some commands onto his computer's keyboard, then turned the monitor her way.

For the next few minutes, she watched the screen, impressed by the unit's layout, furnishings and decor. "It's lovely. It looks like just the sort of place I want. What do I need to do next?"

"We'll need to do a bit of paperwork, and I'll collect your deposit and the first month's rent. Then you'll leave a list of the groceries you want, and we'll take care of the rest."

"How long will it be before I can get into the unit?" She'd long since gotten tired of the chain hotel she was staying in. While the place was serviceable, she thrived on privacy and there was just too much noise and commotion there.

"I can get you in tomorrow, as long as I can get the cleaning crew in there in the next couple of hours."

She breathed a sigh of relief. "Then as soon as I leave here, I'll start packing."

For the next twenty minutes, he worked with her through the property agreement. After she'd signed her name to the document, and selected her desired groceries from the extensive checklist he gave her, she passed his pen back to him.

She sat by as he made calls to the personal shopper and the cleaning crew. Once he was done, he set his phone aside. "You're all set, Ms. Dandridge. Your unit should be ready around 1:00 p.m. tomorrow. Since you put your mobile number on the form, I'll text you the address."

She stood. "Thank you for your help."

He pushed his chair back and stood, as well. "Thank you for your business." Another megawatt smile followed his words.

Turning away lest she started staring at him again, she slung her purse strap over her shoulder and exited.

Back in her car, she let herself feel the glow of his fanboy crush on her for a few moments. Then she banished the thoughts from her mind. Crush or not, she didn't have time for romance right now. The show took up all her free time.

And based on her experiences with men, she wasn't missing anything.

As Campbell moved his stool closer to the bar at the Salty Siren, the wooden feet scraped over the concrete floors. Next to him, his old friend and new brother-in-law, Devon Franklin, drank from a mug of root beer, his eyes trained on one of the big screen televisions. The burger and fries he'd ordered for lunch were on the bar in front of him.

"Sorry I'm late. I see you ordered without me."

Devon shrugged but didn't look away from the

television. "I didn't have time to wait. I gotta be back at the studio by a quarter after one."

"What's got your attention, man?"

Devon sat the mug down. "Haven't you heard? There's a pretty big tropical storm out in the Atlantic right now."

Campbell's eyes widened. September was the peak hurricane season around these parts, but things had been relatively quiet over the last few years. "Good grief. What's going on with it?"

"Just watch the news report, man." Devon kept his gaze on the screen.

Campbell looked, as well, paying close attention to both the on-screen graphics and the words of the local meteorologist.

"Tropical storm Hester is churning in the Atlantic as we speak, folks. She's an angry one, but due to the cool front approaching from the west, we don't expect her to be upgraded or to come on shore for the mainland. However, she does pose the threat of heavy rain, strong winds, rough surf and possible flooding to the islands off the coasts of North Carolina and South Carolina. We expect to see the main impact from the storm over the next twenty-four to thirty-six hours."

Well, shit. Campbell hoped the storm wouldn't cause too much damage. MHI always kept storm preparedness supplies on hand and crews on call this time of year, but the island was abuzz with the cast and crew of *The Shores*, as well as all the extra tourists who'd come in with them.

Devon turned his way after the weather report ended. "It's looking kind of dicey on the weather front. I'd better have the crew film as many scenes as they can this afternoon, in case we have to close down production for a few days."

Shaking his head, Campbell signaled for Maddie, the waitress. "I hope it won't be too bad. With all your people here, plus the folks who came onto the island trying to get on camera when y'all are filming, there are a lot of extra people on the island."

"Yeah. I bet the police and fire people are getting geared up."

"Probably." Thinking MHI should brace for any impact the storm might bring, he fired off a quick text to Savion, letting him know to alert the crew that they might be needed over the next week.

Maddie came over then, and Campbell ordered a buffalo chicken salad and bottled water. After she left, he turned to Devon. "So, I had a meeting with your star earlier today, about a rental unit."

Devon nodded. "So you met with Sierra. She's something, isn't she?"

He whistled. "Yes. She's gorgeous, even more so than she is on-screen."

Devon swallowed a mouthful of food, eyed him closely. "What are you saying, Cam? You trying to get with her?"

He shook his head. "Nah. I mean, yeah, but not

really." He waved his hand in front of him, dismissing the idea. "I don't stand a chance with the 'Ice Queen.'"

With a chuckle, Devon popped a fry into his mouth.

"What does that mean?"

"I'm saying, Cam. Don't sell yourself short. Plus, Sierra isn't nearly as cold as people make her out to be."

"Really?" He folded his arms over his chest. "She seemed all-business this morning."

"That's how she is during business meetings, and that's how she should be. Otherwise no one would take her seriously." He wiped his mouth with a napkin and tossed it aside. "But when you talk to Sierra on a friendly basis, you'll find out she's really sweet."

Cam's thoughts wandered back to the image of her from this morning, which had embedded itself in his mind. She'd been dressed casually, in a pair of skinny jeans, a close-fitting white top and flats. Despite the casual outfit, there was no hiding her curvaceous frame. "I doubt I'll ever get the chance for all of that with her."

"You never know." Devon drained the last of his root beer. "You'll see her again, right?"

He nodded as Maddie slid his salad and drink in front of him. "Yeah. Tomorrow I'm meeting her at her condo with the keys."

"See? Talk to her, and you'll see what I mean."

Campbell nodded, but he still had his doubts.

Parts of him were now even more curious about just who Sierra Dandridge really was. *I guess it's not really fair to make a judgment about her personality, since we just met.* Sure, any sighted man could see she was fine. But he really didn't know anything about her beyond her physical appearance.

He'd make conversation with Sierra and see where it went. After all, as property manager, it was his job to make her feel welcome.

"I can see the gears turning over there," Devon remarked. "What are you up to?"

Shaking his head, Campbell ignored the question and dug into his salad.

Devon folded his arms, waiting. "Cam?"

Campbell chuckled. "Let's just say, when I see her tomorrow, I just may shoot my shot."

Chapter 3

Sierra peered through the rain-slick windshield of her rental car as she drove down the road Wednesday afternoon. The trip from her hotel to the gated community took her halfway across the island, and she was glad the drive was almost over. What had begun as an overcast day with soft, drizzling rain had morphed into a dark, gray-skied downpour. The wipers ran at their fastest speed, giving her enough visibility to operate the car safely. But if the rain increased much more than this, she wouldn't be driving anywhere else today.

Pulling up to the gate at The Glenn, she rolled her window halfway down and gave her name to the guard. The iron gates soon parted, allowing her entry to the complex. Driving through the area, she could see it looked just as picturesque as the photographs in the booklet. The buildings were built from multicolored bricks and accented with stone, and the grounds were manicured with shrubbery and flowers. The images in the brochure had been taken on a sunny day. Today, the plants looked beaten down by the rain and wind, but at least she knew they would look better once the weather cleared up.

She found her building, and pulled into a parking spot in front of it. A tall figure stood on the landing above her, and after she cut the engine, she took a closer look at his face. *Campbell. Good, he's already here.* With her purse on her shoulder, she opened her umbrella and got out of the car. Jogging through the sheets of rain, she climbed the stairs to the second level of the building.

Beneath the canopy of the roof she closed her umbrella, and walked up to the door of unit 202 B, where Campbell stood. Before she could stop herself, she looked him over. He wore a pair of dark slacks and a light blue button-down shirt with the MHI logo on his front pocket. It was a very different look from the suit she'd seen him wearing in the office. *Guess these are his casual work clothes.* He looked just as good dressed this way as he had before, but she pushed that thought out of her mind, telling herself that what he wore and how he looked weren't any of her concern.

She looked back to his face to find him smiling at her.

She blinked, tried to match his smile. Had he seen her staring at him?

Finally, he spoke. "Some weather we're having."

She nodded, relieved. Either he hadn't seen her staring, or had decided not to bring it up. "Yeah. The storm must be pretty darn close."

"Well, let me get you inside before the weather gets worse. The forecast says Hester's gonna hang around for a while." He extracted a single, silver key on an MHI key chain from his pocket.

She watched as he put the key in the lock...or attempted to.

His brow furrowed as he tried a second time to put the key into the lock. "What in the world?" After lifting the key chain in front of his face, he flipped it over and looked at it. He frowned, uttering a single word. "Crap."

Confused, she asked, "What is it?"

"This isn't the right key." He slipped it back into his pocket. "The Glenn is laid out with two condos to each floor, an A unit and a B unit. This is the key to 202 A."

She glanced to the left. "The unit next door? Can't you just lease me that one, since we're already here?"

He shook his head. "Sorry. That unit was rented earlier this morning. Aside from that, your unit is already set up with grocery delivery and everything you requested."

Hopeful, she asked, "You got me a guard?"

He cleared his throat. "Let me revise that. Almost everything you requested is set up in this unit."

She sighed, turning to face the parking lot. Moments later, the wind changed direction, and a spray of fat raindrops hit her in the face.

Wiping away some of the dampness with her hand, she looked to Campbell. "What do you need to do to get the right key? I'd really like to get out of this weather."

"I'll call my intern, Jacob. He rented the other unit, so I'll see what he can tell me."

While he talked on his cell phone, she moved away from the railing, resting her back against the wall in hopes of avoiding another involuntary shower. She tried to eavesdrop discreetly, but all she heard were a few of his deep-voiced words, in between the bouts of wind and rain.

When he disconnected the call, he turned her way. "The key is still at the office, but Jacob had put it away with the paperwork for the other unit. Even though it was rented today, they're not moving in until tomorrow."

"Is that policy? If so, why didn't you put my key with my paperwork?"

He looked sheepish. "That was an error on my part. I had another appointment right after you and I didn't match up your key. Sorry about that."

She pursed her lips. Fine as he was, he seemed a little forgetful. "So, what happens now?"

"Jacob is going to bring the key here."

She blinked several times. "So we're just going to be waiting here, in this weather?"

"I'm sorry, Ms. Dandridge. But it's either that or go sit in our cars until Jacob gets here."

She looked out at the sky. It had grown even darker since she'd arrived, not to mention the heavier rain and the insistent winds. She shook her head. "Nah. I'll wait here. I'm not going back down there."

"I'd hate for you to have to stand up this whole time." He moved closer to her.

Her heart rate sped up for a moment before she realized he was walking past her.

"Can I borrow your umbrella?"

She nodded, handing it off to him.

He opened it, then dashed down the stairs and into the driving rain. She watched as he went to his car, took something out of the back seat and locked up. Holding something close to his body, probably to keep it dry, he jogged back across the sidewalk and up the stairs. Once back on the landing, he closed the umbrella and dangled it over the railing, giving it a little shake. Then he handed the umbrella back to her, along with the thing he'd retrieved and had been clutching to his chest.

She took the soft bundle.

"I always keep a blanket in the car for emergencies. Fold it up a few times so you'll have somewhere to sit."

She did as he asked, and after she'd folded the thick, plaid blanket into a neat rectangle, she placed

it next to the door and took a seat to one side. Looking up at the handsome man towering over her, she
thought she'd follow her mother's sage advice. *When
life gets salty, make margaritas.* Rachel Myers Dandridge was known for her odd little sayings, and that
was probably one of Sierra's favorites. It meant make
the best of a less than ideal situation. To that end,
she patted the blanket next to her. "You can sit here.
There's plenty of room."

He seemed surprised. "Really?"

"Sure. No reason for you to stand up the whole
time, either."

"Even though I got you into this mess?" He seemed
pretty disappointed with himself.

"Everybody makes mistakes, Campbell. Besides,
it's your blanket." She patted the spot again. "Join me."
Even as she asked him to sit, she realized how rare
it was for her to do something like this. She hadn't
earned her nickname by being cordial to men, especially those that inconvenienced her. But something
about Campbell intrigued her. There was something
endearing, and, if she were honest, enticing, about him.

Finally, he nodded, and took a seat next to her.
"Thanks."

"You're welcome." She realized her rectangle
wasn't as long as she'd thought, because now that
he'd sat down, his muscular outer thigh pressed
against her own. A tingle went through her body,
originating from the point of contact and radiating
through her every cell.

* * *

Campbell shifted a bit to his left, trying to put a little distance between them out of respect. But there wasn't much farther he could move without ruining his slacks on the concrete landing, so he stilled. Their thighs were touching, and there was no way she hadn't noticed. If it bothered her, she didn't let on.

The swirling wind and rain continued to pound the building, and he grabbed her umbrella and opened it in front of them to protect them from the elements. The lengthening silence between them made him feel nervous, so he spoke. "Tell me a little about yourself."

She nodded. "Let's see. I'm an only child, and I'm from Los Angeles. My parents still live there. My father owns a welding business and my mother writes historical novels." She paused. "What about you?"

He wanted to hear more about her life, but thought it only fair to divulge a little about his own. "I was born and raised on the island. I'm sure you know my younger sister, Hadley. She's married to Devon. We have an older brother, Savion. MHI is the family business, and we kids took over about six years ago when our parents retired."

"I see." She looked straight ahead, as if focused on the falling rain.

He observed her, enjoying her regal beauty in profile. She was dressed just as casually as the previous day, this time in jeans and a long-sleeved T-shirt.

Her hair was up on top of her head in a messy bun, with a few tendrils hanging around her face. She appeared thoughtful, and he kept quiet to avoid interfering with whatever gears were turning in her mind.

The stormy weather filled the air with the sounds of rain and howling wind, and he kept quiet and listened to the cacophony.

Jacob's car pulled up then, parking a few spots away from Sierra's. As Jacob jogged through the rain with the key, Campbell met him halfway up the stairs.

"Thanks!" He switched keys with Jacob, raising his voice to be heard over the wind. "Now try to get home before the storm gets any worse!"

"Yes, sir!" Jacob ran back to his car, and soon pulled off.

His shirt damp with rain, Campbell returned to the door and slipped the key into the lock. Turning it, he swung open the door. "Welcome to your unit, Ms. Dandridge."

She started to get up, and he offered his hand to assist her. On her feet, she smiled as she passed him, entering the condo.

He gathered the blanket and the umbrella and followed her inside, closing the door. The sound of the rainstorm was now buffered, but he could still hear the rain and wind. "Let me give you a quick tour, and I'll be out of your hair."

"Okay." She trailed him around the unit and let him show her all the features and amenities it had.

"You've got plenty of space to stretch out here." He showed her the living room, kitchen/dining combo, the hall bathroom and the guest bedroom. In the master suite, he showed her the king-size bed and the attached bathroom, complete with soaking tub and separate shower. She lay across the bed for a moment, as if to test it, and he turned away to keep his thoughts from going in that direction.

As if sensing his discomfort, she sat up and got on her feet again. "Everything looks wonderful. Anything else you want to show me?"

He gestured for her to follow him back up the narrow hallway. "There's a terrace off the dining room. You can access it by those glass doors. Nice views of the inlet from out there." He pointed at them as they returned to the main living area. "But you'll probably want to wait for better weather to check that out."

She chuckled. "Definitely."

It was the first time he'd heard her laugh. The sound, brief as it had been, seemed to brighten his world. He walked over to the stainless steel double-door refrigerator in the kitchen, and opened both doors. "As you can see, our shoppers have stocked your fridge with everything you requested from the list."

She came over and inspected the contents, grabbing a Gala apple from a shelf. "This is great." She closed the doors, then went to the sink to rinse the apple.

"That's about it. Sorry again about the whole key mix-up."

She'd searched out a knife and cutting board, and was busy cutting up her apple. "It's okay."

"I'm gonna head out and leave you to relax, then." He bundled up his blanket, tucked it under his arm and walked toward the door. As he swung it open, greeted by the fierce winds, he thought he heard her call his name.

"Campbell. Wait."

He turned around to face her in the doorway. "Did you call me? Do you need something else?"

She stood by the kitchen counter, with the slices of apple on a napkin. "I don't need anything else, no."

He shrugged. "See ya."

"Wait."

He turned back again. "I thought you said you didn't need anything else?"

She looked conflicted. "I don't. But…I don't think you should be going out there in this weather. We've been here for a little while, and it's been getting worse this whole time."

He watched her face, and saw the lines of concern there. While he didn't know what had given rise to her concern for him, he couldn't help but be flattered by it. "Let me take a look out there."

He took a few steps out onto the landing, to ascertain conditions below them. The wind and rain were still steadily pounding the building, and the trees below appeared to be dancing as they waved their branches in time. His eyes swept over the parking lot, and he saw the deepening puddles forming on the black concrete. Instinct told him to walk to the other end of the landing, so he pulled the door shut gently and strolled to the right, past the door to the A unit. From that end of the landing, he craned his neck a bit to get a view of the inlet.

Sure enough, the banks of the inlet had disappeared beneath the rising water. This part of the island was particularly low lying, but bordered Cooper Inlet instead of the Atlantic Ocean. When flooding happened here, it was often due to too much rain overflowing the inlet as opposed to seawater breaching the island's curved seawall.

She's right. I can't go out in this. Based on what he could see, and the pattern he recognized from living most of his life in Sapphire Shores, this side of the island would be under a good foot or so of water, and soon.

He returned to her unit then, and found her standing in the open door, as if she'd come out to look for him. "Where did you go?"

He pointed. "Around to the end of the landing. The inlet's flooding, so you're right. I probably shouldn't be driving."

A soft smile met his words. "Good. Then come back inside out of this madness."

Once they were both inside again, he sat on one end of the tan sofa. "I appreciate this, Ms. Dandridge."

"Call me Sierra."

"If you insist." The movie fan inside him did back flips. *I'm on a first-name basis with Sierra Dandridge!*

She brought her sliced apple over to the coffee table and set it down. "Do you want something to eat or drink?"

"I'll take a bottle of water, please."

She returned with two chilled bottles and passed him one. Cracking hers open, she took a seat on the opposite end of the sofa. "You've been through these storms before, right?"

"Sure. We've been through at least twenty that had some level of impact. Fran, Floyd, Isabel. Why do you ask?"

"How long do they usually last?"

He shrugged. "Storms, a day or two. It's the aftermath that can drag on and on."

She looked thoughtful. "No telling how long you'll have to stay, then."

He winked. "Nope."

Chapter 4

Sierra stood by the glass doors in the dining room, assessing the scene outside. Just as Campbell had mentioned earlier, the waters of Cooper Inlet were escaping. The inlet, about two miles away, had already begun to swell onto the road running next to it. The storm still raged on, with the wind and rain swirling beneath the darkened sky.

With a sigh, she walked away from the door and back into the living room area. The gilded analog clock on the wall showed her that the dinner hour approached, but the rumbling in her stomach told her it had arrived.

She looked to Campbell, who was still sitting on the end of the sofa. He had his phone out, and had been staring at it for a while. The screen glow illuminated his face in the dimness of the room.

Moving toward the kitchen, she called out to him. "Campbell, are you hungry?"

He glanced up. "Sorry, did you say something?"

"I asked if you're hungry."

He nodded. "Do you need help cooking?"

She flipped the wall switch by the fridge, flooding the kitchen with soft, white light. "Not right now. What's got your attention over there?"

"I'm reading a book. I've got one of those e-reader apps on my phone."

Her brow crinkled. "What are you reading?" Opening the refrigerator, she scanned the shelves for the bundle of fresh herbs she'd seen there earlier.

"The collected poems of Langston Hughes."

She stopped midreach, angling her head so she could look at him. "Really?"

He looked up then, meeting her eyes. "Yes, really. Why do you look so shocked?"

"It's just…I've never met a man who read poetry. At least not one who would openly admit it."

He shrugged. "To be honest, it's not just 'reading poetry.' Langston's the man. Even all these years after his death, his words still resonate."

Recovered a bit from her initial shock, she grabbed the plastic clamshell case holding the herbs and set them on the counter. "It's refreshing to meet someone who shares my opinion. I adore Langston's work."

He watched her, as if seeing her with new eyes. "No kidding. What's your favorite of his poems?"

She thought about it as she removed unsalted butter, a loin of pork and a pound of fresh brussels sprouts from the fridge. "I'd have to say 'Mother to Son,' with 'Harlem' being a close second."

He tilted his head to one side, appearing thoughtful. "I see. Those are definitely seminal works of his."

She washed her hands with the lemon-scented dish soap and dried them on a checked towel. Grabbing three russet potatoes from the wire basket on the kitchen counter, she set to work peeling them. With a glance over all the food she'd set out, she thought she should revise her earlier statement. "Listen, why don't you come in here. I think this will go faster if I have an extra set of hands, and we can keep talking while we cook."

"No problem." He placed the phone facedown on the coffee table and came to the kitchen. She inched to the left, so he could access the sink, and while he washed his hands, she kept working the vegetable peeler, turning the potato in her hand.

As the peel fell in a perfect spiral, she set it down and reached for the second one.

He dried his hands and asked, "What do you want me to do?"

She gestured toward the rest of the food sitting on the counter. "Grab a deep roaster, and halve those sprouts, please."

"You got it." He searched the lower cabinets for the roaster.

As he bent, her greedy eyes devoured the sight of his muscled thighs and the perfect shape of his rear end. The man was built like a warrior, and looking at him now, she couldn't help wondering about his "spear."

He stood then, having located a large, white ceramic roaster. After he set that on the counter and got a knife and cutting board, he began working on the sprouts, splitting them with precision and expertise.

As she cubed her peeled potatoes on a separate board, the room grew quiet, save for the sounds of the storm and of their knives striking the boards. To break the silence, she glanced at him. "You never told me your favorite Langston Hughes poem."

He chuckled. "You never asked."

She gave him a sidelong glance. "I'm asking now. So, tell me."

After sliding a handful of halved sprouts off the cutting board and into a colander, he set the knife down. "I love the two you mentioned. But my absolute favorite is 'April Rain Song.'"

She searched her mind for a moment, before the words to that poem came back to her. "Oh, yes. The one with the rain kissing you…"

He turned around to face her.

Their gazes met, locked.

Something lay behind the dark pools of his eyes, something she couldn't name. Whatever it was, it made her knees tremble. To steady herself, she pressed the small of her back against the edge of the counter.

He began reciting the poem, drawing each word out, the way the men around here tended to do. She'd heard the words before, but never in this deep, molasses-thick drawl. With each word, she felt tingles race over the surface of her skin.

When he'd finished, she drew in a deep breath to fill her empty lungs. "Wow."

"So you enjoyed my recitation?"

She nodded. "You certainly put a lot of…um… feeling into it."

A slight smile turned up the corners of his full lips. "That's the only way to do it when you're reciting the work of a true master."

She swallowed, nodded again. What she didn't say was that he'd shown her a whole new side to the piece. She'd never considered that poem sensual in any way, until just now. Hearing him recite it gave the poem an erotic edge she never would have ascribed to it before. Whether Mr. Hughes had written such undertones into it, she didn't know. But she did know she'd never hear that poem the same way again.

Her stomach growled a loud, hungry protest. She pressed her palms over it, as if that would muffle the sound.

Campbell reacted with a short, rumbling laugh. "We'd better get back to cooking. Your stomach is about to stage a coup." He moved closer to her, then past her to rinse the sprouts in the sink.

Feeling her cheeks warm, she blew out a breath. "Sorry about that."

He waved her off while he ran a stream of water over the sprouts. "No big deal. Hunger is a natural thing, nothing to be ashamed of."

I'm hungry, alright. He had no idea she was fighting down more than one appetite. It seemed like ages since she'd been in the company of a man so handsome, thoughtful and intelligent. Her sometimes crazy filming schedule didn't leave much free time for dating and relationships. This was the first time in almost six months she'd been alone with any man.

And if he stayed much longer, looking as delicious as he did, she had no idea where things would go between them.

After she recovered her senses, she set to work assembling the food for cooking. Then she placed the roaster, with the seasoned pork loin resting atop a bed of potatoes and sprouts, into the oven. "Now we just have to wait for it to get done."

She rinsed her hands in the sink, ridding them of the olive oil she'd massaged into the meat, then toweled them dry. As she shut off the water, her traitorous stomach growled…again.

"Are you gonna be alright until it's ready?" With his tone light and teasing, he looked her way.

She smiled. "I think I'll be fine."

Waiting for the food would be the easy part.

Keeping her hands off him would be a whole different matter.

* * *

As night fell over Cooper Inlet, Campbell found himself back on the sofa with Sierra. They'd returned there after finishing the delicious meal they'd made. The main difference between now and earlier was that she seemed a little more relaxed, and had chosen to sit on the middle cushion rather than on the opposite end of the sofa.

Outside, the wind had calmed somewhat, but the rain showed no signs of stopping. By his estimate, he wasn't likely to be going anywhere before tomorrow morning, at the earliest.

She'd turned on the television and surfed to an episode of *Mysteries at the Museum*. He half watched the show while continuing to page through the poetry book on his phone. She sat close enough now for him to pick up the feminine scent emanating from her. He couldn't tell if it was perfume or shampoo, or a combination of the many grooming products women tended to use. Whatever the case, she smelled of bright citrus and spicy cinnamon, and the combination intoxicated him.

During the commercial break, she looked his way. "This show is a trip. They always find the weirdest artifacts with the craziest backstories."

He nodded. "Yeah. I've seen a couple of episodes, and it is pretty wild."

She stood then. "Do you want any more food? If not, I'm about to put it away."

He patted his stomach and shook his head. "I'm full. It tasted great, by the way."

She winked. "You get some of the credit, since you were my sous-chef." Turning, she walked to the kitchen.

He watched her every step, hypnotized by the sway of her ample hips. The way she walked seemed like an art form, a manifestation of her confidence and femininity. She wasn't twisting or strutting; this was her natural gait. It was the physical manifestation of who she was, or at least it seemed that way based on his limited knowledge of her. Whatever it was, that certain something about her was what made her so attractive, and made her so talented as an actress. He'd seen this mysterious quality of hers play out on-screen many times before, and in no film had it been played up so much as in *Waltz at Midnight*.

She moved around the kitchen, putting the leftover food in glass containers and tucking it into the fridge. When she returned, she sat down and tucked her bare feet beneath her hips.

His brow lifted. *Am I imagining it, or is she sitting closer to me now?* Wordlessly, he placed his hand palm down on the sofa. Sure enough, there wasn't enough room now for him to spread his fingers.

Lifting his hand again, he rested it on his thigh, fighting back a smile. It was possible she didn't realize how close she'd sat. It was also possible she'd purposely moved into his personal bubble. Either way, he wasn't going to be the one to mention it.

They were in her place, and whatever happened tonight would be on her terms.

By now, the show had returned from the break, and she fell right in, watching it with interest. He, on the other hand, set aside his phone and contented himself with watching her. As entertaining as the show was, he found Sierra even more interesting.

She seemed to notice his regard, because she turned her large, sparkling dark eyes his way and asked, "What is it?"

"Sorry, I didn't mean to make you uncomfortable."

She shrugged. "I'm not uncomfortable, really. I just couldn't help noticing you staring at me."

"I was just thinking about something. Remember how I told you *Waltz at Midnight* is one of my favorite movies of all time?"

A soft smile tilted her lips. "Yes, I remember, and I appreciate you saying that."

"I meant it." He scratched his chin. "Can I ask you a question about that movie?"

"Sure."

"Do you feel you have anything in common with your character?"

"You mean Reva Lane, the jewel thief better known as the Midnight Shadow?" She chuckled, then made a dramatic gesture with both hands. "Well, I've never knocked over a jewelry store, if that's what you're asking."

He laughed. "No, that's not what I mean. I mean

her attitude, her outlook on things. Do you share anything like that with her?"

Her gaze shifted, as if she were looking outside at the falling rain. "I'd like to think I'm as fearless and intelligent as she is." She eyed him. "What made you ask that question?"

"I see a little of her in you. At least I think I do, based on our limited interactions."

She shifted a little closer to him, changing position until she sat cross-legged, right next to him. Their thighs were now touching again, just as they had when they were sitting on the landing earlier. "Care to elaborate on that?"

"I see you as guarded, closed off."

She pursed her lips.

Sensing her annoyance, he held up his hand. "Wait, hear me out. I also see you as confident and self-assured. That's probably what stood out to me the most about the character, and I saw it again in Della's the other day."

"What do you mean?"

"I saw you with your costar. I can tell she's not your favorite person, but you kept it very professional. At least from what I saw." He stretched his arms over his head, to shake off some of the stiffness from sitting so long in one position. "I did leave before the scene finished filming, but I'm gonna assume you didn't go upside her head."

She laughed then, releasing a full, diaphragm-deep sound that brightened his whole world. When she finally recovered, she shook her head, the mirth still visible in her eyes. "You're a mess!"

"But I'm right, though."

She giggled. "Yeah. I'm not too fond of Mia, but I'm not about to jeopardize my career for her or anyone else."

He smiled. "See, that's what I mean. You've got your head on straight, your priorities are in order and your path laid out. You're out here going for what you want without waiting for permission. I respect that."

The humor dancing in her eyes morphed into something else. She held his gaze. "Do you really think that? Or is this just flattery?"

"It's the truth. Yeah, I'll admit I feel like a teenage boy who got pulled onstage with his favorite singer right now." *Damn. Didn't mean to say that aloud.* He ran a hand over his face. "But I meant every word I said."

The soft smile on her face grew even bigger. "Wow."

He smiled back, still trying to read that look in her eyes. *What is she thinking right now?*

A moment later, she leaned toward him. Her small hand came up to cup his jaw. "You're quite the charmer, Campbell Monroe."

"Not really." He couldn't tear his eyes away from hers. His face tingled beneath the warmth of her touch. "I'm just honest."

She tilted her head, letting her eyes drift closed as her lips formed that unmistakable pucker shape.

He didn't know how they'd gotten here, but he wasn't about to turn down an invitation like that. He placed a hand on her shoulder, then gently touched his lips to hers. Her lips were plump, soft and made for kissing. They tasted of some fruit-flavored lip gloss, and as he gave her a series of little pecks on the lips, he got a taste of it every few seconds.

She responded by moving her hand to grip the back of his neck, and letting her mouth fall open. He closed his eyes, too, prepared to savor her and this moment. Their tongues mated, stroking against each other as their upper bodies pressed closer together. He found the interior of her mouth just as sweet as her lips had been. He embraced her, cradling her in his arms and pulling her onto his lap as the kiss deepened. She moaned into his mouth, and the sound lit the fire in his blood. Her body seemed to fit perfectly against his, and holding her felt as natural and right as breathing.

He felt her take a sharp inhale, then jerk away, abruptly breaking the seal of their lips. He opened his eyes just in time to see her scoot off his lap and stand. Looking up at her, he frowned. "What happened? Is something wrong?"

She brought her arms up, crossing them over her chest with her hands on her shoulders. Her gaze retreating, she simply shook her head. "I can't."

He felt his brow knitting. He couldn't recall ever being so confused by a woman's actions.

But before he could say anything more, she turned

and jogged down the hallway. Moments later, he heard her bedroom door slam.

With a sigh, he fell back against the sofa cushions. *What in the world just happened?*

Chapter 5

When Sierra woke up Thursday morning, the sunlight streaming through the white lace curtains let her know she'd slept later than she intended. Groggy, she rubbed her eyes and sat up, running a hand over her wild locks.

It took her a few moments to figure out where she was. She'd gotten so accustomed to sleeping in her hotel suite that waking up in the condo felt a bit jarring. She blinked a few times, letting her vision adjust to the brightness as her mind came awake.

Her eyes widened as she remembered last night.

Last night.

Her hand flew to cover her mouth.

I kissed Campbell. Holy crap.

She'd kissed Campbell, alright. And then run away and locked herself in the bedroom for the rest of the night. She'd tossed and turned for quite a while, but the pounding rain had eventually lulled her to sleep.

He hadn't followed her, hadn't knocked on the door to see if she were alright. And she was glad of that, because if he had come, she wouldn't have known what to say to him. That's why she ran away. He'd just gotten through telling her how intelligent and self-assured he thought she was, and yet, after kissing him, she couldn't formulate a coherent sentence.

She swiveled her head to the right, looking at the closed bedroom door. If he had any sense, he was still in the condo. Only a fool would have gone out in that kind of weather.

She threw back the covers, slipping out of bed. Dressed in the camisole and panties she'd been wearing under her clothes yesterday, she walked to the door, feeling the chill of the hardwood floors beneath her bare feet with each step. Arriving at the door, she gave the handle a slow turn and cracked the door open.

The first thing she noticed was the sound of his snores. *He must be sleeping good.* The log-sawing sound rattled the air in an otherwise silent space. Peering through the crack, she saw him stretched out on the sofa, with the plaid blanket draped over his body. He was on his back, his head propped up on one of the armrests. The way he lay, he faced the hallway and her bedroom door.

Shutting the door just as silently as she'd opened it, she stood with her back against it for a minute. *What am I going to do?* She knew she'd have to leave the room eventually; she had to eat. The subject of last night was bound to come up. What was she going to say to him?

She walked to the glazed mahogany dresser, grabbing her phone from the top. It was after nine. Jazmin should be up by now. As she dialed the number, she caught a glimpse of herself in the mirror and cringed. She'd forgotten to tie her hair up last night, and now it resembled a partially woven basket sitting crooked on top of her head. She balanced the phone between her face and her shoulder as it rang, and ran her hands over her hair to tame it.

"Hello?" Jazmin's voice filled her ear as she answered the call. "What's up, Sierra?"

Speaking in a quiet, but urgent tone, she said, "Jazzy. I got a problem."

"I know, girl. Isn't it flooded over there where you are?"

"I don't know." She glanced toward the window then, realizing she hadn't even thought to look outside. "If it is, that's a problem, but that's not what I meant."

"If you're worried about not showing up on set, don't be. Devon shut down production for the day so the crew can help with cleanup."

She rested her face in her hands. Jazmin was a natural problem solver, but sometimes her tendency to try to predict the problem got on Sierra's nerves. "Jazzy, will you please hush? This is a *man* problem."

"It's a what?"

She sighed. "A man problem."

"I just wanted to make sure I heard you correctly. Why are you whispering?"

"Because my problem is still here in the condo with me."

"Still there, as in he was there all night?" Jazmin's tone held a mixture of amusement and shock.

"Yes, he was, but—"

Jazmin cut her off. "Ooh, congrats, girl! I know you haven't gotten any of the good stuff in a hot minute! Was it good? Did he blow ya back out?"

Flopping down on the end of the bed, Sierra couldn't help rolling her eyes. "Jazmin, chill. He was here last night because of the storm. We didn't do it."

Sympathy replaced her previous jubilation. "Oh, girl. I'm sorry. So that's the problem. You didn't get any…again. We gotta get you back in the game, sis."

"Jazzy, if I was sitting in the room with you, I'd have popped you by now. Just hush and listen. He came here yesterday to give me the keys to my unit. He ended up bringing the wrong key, and we had to wait on the landing for his intern to bring the right one. By then the weather was too bad for me to send him out in it, so he stayed here."

"Okay, you've said 'he' like a hundred times. Who is he?"

"His name is Campbell. He's the property manager for the company that owns the condo complex I'm staying in."

Jazmin was silent for a few long moments. "Wait a minute. You mean Campbell Monroe?"

"You know him?"

"Girl, yeah! His company owns just about every residential property on the island. Plus, he's friends with Devon. I've seen him on the set a few times." She paused again. "He's fine, girl."

"You don't have to tell me that. I've been with him since early yesterday afternoon." It was that fineness, combined with the charm he exuded, that had led her to kiss him in the first place. "But I don't have time for involvement right now, no matter how fine he is."

"Okay. So, I'm confused." Jazmin blew out a loud breath. "If he's been at your house all night, and y'all didn't do anything, and you didn't *want* to do anything, then what's the problem?"

She took a deep breath. "I said we didn't do 'it,' but I didn't say we didn't do anything." She searched for the right words. "We kissed. Or rather, I kissed him."

She could hear Jazmin clapping. "Girl, you are a walking contradiction. You just spent the last ten minutes saying he's a problem, and now you tell me you kissed him? Make up your mind!"

Sierra let her head drop back in frustration. "I created the problem. We were talking, I got carried away, and now I'm sitting in my bedroom, afraid to go out of it."

"Why? It's gonna be awkward, we both know that. But you're being ridiculous. It was just a little kiss."

"I wouldn't describe it as a 'little kiss' by any means, Jazmin." Memories of last night sprang up again. She'd relished being in his strong arms, feeling his lips against hers. She hadn't intended to open her mouth, but she'd been so intoxicated and caught up in the moment, it just happened. And she'd enjoyed every second of it. But she didn't dare give voice to her thoughts. "I just hope I didn't give him the wrong impression."

"It was a kiss, Sierra. Nobody said you had to marry the brotha just because you kissed him." Jazmin chuckled. "Although, you could use a little you-know-what."

"Oh, quit." Sierra giggled in spite of her mood. "I'm going to take a shower. Bye, Jazmin."

"Okay, girl. Let me know how this turns out, though."

She disconnected the call, shaking her head at her friend's comments. Still, she had gleaned one truth from Jazmin: a kiss could mean as much or as little as she wanted it to mean.

And I've decided it doesn't mean a thing.

The smell of coffee brewing awoke Campbell from his sleep. He didn't hear any rain, so he assumed the storm had passed.

Sitting up on the sofa, he started to stretch, but stopped midway due to the stiffness in his neck and shoulders. As he stifled a yawn, he looked around the room for any sign of Sierra. He didn't see her, so he tossed off the blanket, got up and trudged to the hallway bathroom.

When he emerged, having taken care of his needs, and washed his face, he found her sitting in the armchair across from the sofa, with a magazine on her lap. She looked up when he walked in.

"Good morning."

She tilted her head to the side. "Almost afternoon. But good morning."

He chuckled. "Sorry I slept so late. I must have been pretty tired."

"I've been up for a bit. I went out to get my bags from the car, then took a shower and changed." She closed the magazine and set it on the coffee table. "After that I started the coffee maker and went to find my latest issue of *Newsweek*."

"So, you've been outside, then." He glanced toward the front window. "How bad is it out there?"

She shrugged. "Not too bad. The far end of the parking lot, closest to the inlet, is flooded."

"You know, if you'd have woken me up, I would have carried your bags up for you."

She waved him off. "Don't worry about it. You were sleeping so peacefully, I didn't want to disturb you."

"Have you eaten?"

She gestured to the mug of coffee sitting on the table. "Coffee is made from beans. Does that count?"

He shook his head. "No dice. It's made from beans but it's a beverage, not a food." He clapped his hands together. "Why don't you let me whip us up some omelets?"

One of her flawless brows lifted. "You cook?"

"Yeah. I'm in my thirties, and at some point, it was either learn to cook or spend all my time ordering takeout." He started walking toward the kitchen. "Do you have a favorite type of omelet?"

She shook her head. "No. I'll leave the particulars up to you."

"Got it." In the kitchen, he washed and dried his hands, then began assembling everything he would need. He buttered a large skillet and set it on medium heat on the stovetop, then quickly chopped a green pepper, a red pepper, a sweet onion and a few strips of grilled chicken breast.

She entered the kitchen while he was whisking eggs with a dash of milk. Setting her mug on the dispenser of the single-cup coffee brewer, she set the machine to make her a second cup. She looked around at the ingredients he'd pulled out. "This looks promising."

"It'll be the best omelet you've ever had." He winked, then ladled some of the eggs into the bubbling butter in the pan. On top of that, he tossed veggies, chicken and a healthy handful of sharp cheddar cheese.

She lingered by his side while her coffee brewed, and he stole a glance or two as he took care of the omelets. "Can you grab a couple of plates, please?"

"Sure." She reached to the upper cabinets and pulled down two white ceramic plates.

When they were at the table with their omelets and two tall glasses of orange juice, he waited while she cut into hers. After she took the first bite, he saw the satisfied smile spread over her face. But he wanted to hear her say it, so he asked, "How is it?"

"Great. Thanks for cooking."

"You're welcome." He dug into his own food.

They made small talk between bites, and by the time he set their empty plates in the sink, he realized she had no intention of bringing up what had happened last night. He strolled to the sofa where she sat and asked, "Are we going to talk about last night?"

With a sidelong glance and a flat tone, she said, "No."

He sat down on the opposite end, assuming she'd want the distance. "Why not, Sierra?"

Her long sigh followed his question. "There's nothing to talk about."

"I think there is."

"It was just a little harmless kiss." She stared toward the television, even though it wasn't turned on.

"If that's the case, then why don't you want to address it?"

She spun around then. "What exactly should I be addressing, Campbell?"

He looked her right in the eyes. "Why you pulled away so suddenly. Why you ran out of here the way you did. What you meant when you said, 'I can't.'"

She pursed her lips tightly. "You've known me all of two days. I don't think I owe you any explanations, Campbell."

"You do recall that *you* kissed *me*, right?" He placed strategic emphasis on his words, to remind her of just how things had gone down. "That's the only reason I'm asking. You went from wanting to kiss me one moment, to running away the next."

She shrugged, as if it meant nothing. "The fact remains. You don't know me, and I'm not obligated to explain myself to you."

He sat back against the cushions, more confused than before. He'd wanted to think he was getting to know the real Sierra Dandridge, the woman behind the many roles she'd played. Now he knew better. The Ice Queen thing was real, because he was starting to feel the chill rolling off her. "You know, you're right, Sierra. You don't owe me anything. You let me stay here during the storm, and I made you breakfast. Guess that makes us even, huh?"

Her expression changed then, and she looked conflicted. "I didn't mean to be—"

He stopped her midsentence. "Don't apologize for being who you are." He stood then, and started folding up his blanket. Then he walked around the room, gathering his wallet, keys and phone. "I'll get out of your hair, since I've clearly worn out my welcome."

She frowned. "You don't have to rush off."

He went to the front door and opened it, looking outside. "The sun's out, and I don't see anything too bad from here."

"The news this morning said there's localized flooding and downed tree limbs and debris on some of the roads." She stood then, lacing her fingers in front of her. "It may not be safe."

He watched her, shaking his head. She was as fickle as the weather on the island. One minute as warm as a summer day, and the next minute colder than a polar bear's toenails. "I'll take my chances out there. I've dealt with hurricanes and tropical storms before. You, on the other hand, are a whole different issue."

And before she could say anything else, he walked out, shutting the door behind him.

Behind the wheel of his car, he had just enough time to see her open the door before he backed out of the parking space and drove away.

As he headed south and west toward home, he encountered a few blocked roadways, forcing him to take a longer route. Along the way, he chastised himself for thinking there could be something between him and Sierra. He'd let his feelings as a fan of her work bleed over into the reality of the situation. She was a client, and nothing more. No matter how beautiful and savvy he found her, there was no real reason to believe they could have anything more than a business relationship.

This was the problem with women. Just when he thought he understood one of them, she'd introduce a new variable to the equation. He'd been with his ex-wife for five years, and in hindsight, he could see that he'd never really known her, either. Even sharing a home, a bed and a life with her hadn't revealed all her secrets.

Sierra had shown him who she was, and he knew he should just accept it.

But parts of him still wondered if he would ever get the chance to rediscover the heat he sensed in her, burning deep beneath her cool exterior. He'd gotten a taste of it when she kissed him, and now, he didn't think he'd ever forget it.

Chapter 6

Sierra spent most of the day curled up on the arm-chair in the living room, going over her script for *The Shores*. Even though she didn't know when filming would resume, she decided that reading up on her lines would be a better use of her time than moping around all day.

After finishing her third read-through and her second cup of hot tea, she set the script aside and got up. It felt good to be on her feet again, and she took a moment to stretch before going to the kitchen to put away her mug.

On the way back, she passed the sofa. Her eyes moved to the spot that Campbell had occupied only hours earlier. She sighed. Riding out the storm with him had been crazy, unexpected and, at times, pleasant. She'd enjoyed his company and his conversation. But while she felt she'd done the right thing by not sending him home during the storm, she wondered where this turn of events would lead.

She scoffed as she went down the hall to the master bedroom. *What does it matter? I'm pretty sure he never wants to talk to me again.* Making things awkward between them hadn't been her intention, but that's just what she'd done. Searching through her clothes for a jacket, she thought back on how frustrated he'd seemed that morning.

I guess I understand why he wanted answers. The thing was, she didn't have any answers for him. At least, not any he'd find satisfactory. The kiss had been unplanned, and her bolting from him had been the natural reaction when she'd finally come to her senses. Explaining the whys of that, though, just wasn't going to happen.

Locating the black windbreaker she'd been looking for, she slipped it on over her black tee. Once she'd added black leather boots that extended over the knees of her black jeans, she added a bright red beret atop her hair. To her mind, the pop of color kept her from looking as if she were about to attend a funeral.

With her keys, wallet and phone in her jacket pockets, she stepped out onto the landing. The warm air still held some of the dampness from the rain, but the sky was much brighter. The sun peeked through the thick, light gray clouds.

Looking down over the railing, she saw that the front lot where she'd parked was fine. The few deep puddles she'd seen earlier had either dried up or been drawn down into the storm drains.

She turned and locked the door, then walked down the steps. On the ground again, she went to the side of the building and glanced around back. There was still a good amount of standing water near buildings four and five. Thankfully, she didn't have to go that way. Deciding to take advantage of the fresh air and get a little exercise in, she set out on foot, walking west down the road toward Tracemore Plaza.

She stepped over several fallen limbs on the sidewalk, and dodged more than a few piles of leaves and debris, as well as a few puddles. The flat boots were comfortable to walk in, and kept her feet dry as she made the trip. She inhaled the rain-scented air, then blew it out through her lips. She'd spent only a day and a half trapped inside, but it had seemed much longer. Now she relished being outside, with the warm sun caressing her face and the birds' songs ringing in her ears.

She arrived at the plaza and let her eyes sweep over the cluster of businesses located on the manicured strip of pavement and grass. The picture there was similar to what she'd seen elsewhere in the neighborhood: scattered branches and leaves, windswept litter and rain-slick pavement. The accessories boutique on one end of the plaza wasn't open. When she went to the door to read the sign, she saw that the owners had closed the place due to "a storm-related power outage."

Della's was on the far end, and a loud buzzing sound, as well as a crowd gathered around the front door, drew her attention. She made her way down the walk, and as she approached, she saw the large tree that had fallen there. The tree blocked three parking spaces, and one end of it rested against Della's front door.

She discovered the buzzing was coming from a chain saw, wielded by a muscular man in a white tank top and jeans. She stood out of the way of the flying sawdust and watched as he expertly divided the tree into sections.

Della walked over then. "Hey, Ms. Sierra. How'd you make out in this storm?"

"Just a little water in the parking lot. Nothing too serious."

She gestured to the tree. "You see what happened here. We built in this area very purposely, and left as many of the existing trees as we could." She shook her head. "When the storm knocked this one down, the old girl took the electric line down with her. Knocked out power on this whole block."

"Uh-oh. Sorry to hear that, but I'm glad my power stayed on." While she spoke, she kept her eyes trained on the chain saw–wielding brotha. While she couldn't see his face, something about him seemed... familiar.

* * *

Having turned the entire tree into a pile of firewood, he stood up and lifted his safety goggles.

The moment he turned to look where she and Della stood, Sierra's breath caught in her throat.

Campbell? Of all the things she could have imagined him doing, and there were plenty, using a chain saw wasn't one of them. But now, she doubted she'd ever get the image of his bare arms and shoulders working, his hands controlling the equipment like a pro, out of her mind.

When he saw her, he nodded in her direction, his expression flat. "I'm gonna get the guys to help me stack this up, Della."

"Thank you, Cam." She smiled at him, then turned back to Sierra. "What's wrong, honey? You look pretty stricken."

Shaking herself free, Sierra laughed it off. "Sorry. I just checked out for a minute."

"Well, anyhow, I'm glad to have Campbell and Savion nearby. I just called them up and they came right on over. Even brought a few of their friends along to help."

"You've probably known them for a while," Sierra remarked, watching the group of men haul the logs around the side of the building.

"Yep. I've known those Monroe boys since they were knee-high to a piano bench. Good boys, always have been. Love 'em like my own." She patted Sierra's shoulder. "You didn't come down to eat, did you? Power's still on the fritz."

She shook her head. "No. Just wanted to get out of the house. You know, get some fresh air, clear my mind."

Della nodded, a knowing look in her eyes. "Some things press on your mind for good reason." With a wink, Della slipped away to supervise the guys.

Sierra started walking back the way she'd come, wanting to avoid running into Campbell.

She'd taken about five steps before he tapped her on the shoulder. "Hey."

Stopping, she glanced back at him. "Hey."

"Headed home?" He pulled off a pair of thick canvas gloves, shoving them into the pockets of his jeans.

She nodded. "Yeah. I just came out to get some air."

"Why don't you let me drop you off? I'll pass your place on my way home."

"I don't want to trouble you."

"It's no trouble." He looked into her eyes, and she thought she saw a ghost of a smile.

She acquiesced. "Okay. Thanks."

He started walking, and she followed him across the parking lot to his car.

Campbell let the top down on his convertible once he and Sierra were belted in, then slowly backed out of the parking spot. Once on the road, he enjoyed the feeling of the wind on his face.

He glanced at his silent passenger and shook his head. She seemed to be making a point of not looking in his direction. Placing his own focus back on the road, he spoke. "I know you don't like me asking you questions, but could I ask just one?"

"If it's not pertaining to the last day and a half, go ahead."

He shook his head. "Okay. So, in terms of your career, I see you playing the same kinds of roles all the time. Don't get me wrong, you're a brilliant actress. But you're always playing variations of the same character."

"This is the longest question ever."

"Do you feel like you've been typecast?"

Even without taking his eyes off the road, he knew she was looking directly at him. "What made you ask that?"

"I always see you mentioned in the media as an 'ice queen.'" He'd experienced a bit of the chill for himself this morning, but he left that out. "Even if you don't follow reviews and stuff, you have to know how that image of you is always being pushed." He stopped at a red light. "So, do you feel you've been typecast?"

She gave a slow nod. "Yes. Every single day." She ran a hand over her hair, then blew out a breath. "But how can I complain, really? I've made a great career playing the cold antiheroine or villainess over and over again."

The light changed and he pulled through the intersection. "Then we have something in common."

"I don't understand what you mean." She sounded genuinely confused.

"In a way, I feel typecast. I'm not an actor, but my family sees me a certain way, and it's very hard to get them to change their views." He made the left turn off the road and into the driveway, approaching the security gate to The Glenn. After getting buzzed in by the guard, he pulled through the open gate. "See, at work, they think I'm lazy, when I'm really just unfocused. Property management isn't all that exciting, but I get my work done. I care about the family business just as much as they do, but they never see that."

"Can't they see the evidence? I mean, if your work is getting done, they should be able to tell."

"Normally they would be able to tell. But since the studio opened, the influx of people on the island has easily doubled my workload. So, no matter how fast or hard I work, I'm going to be a bit behind for a while."

"What about your intern?"

"I have two, but they're both part-time."

"I see." She cocked her head, looking thoughtful. "Is it just work? I mean, does your family have you pigeonholed in other ways?"

He parked in front of her condo building and cut

the engine. Now that he wasn't driving, he could really focus on the conversation. "If it was just work, that would be bad enough. But they've also decided who they think I am when it comes to relationships."

The rise of her brow indicated her interest.

"I'm a divorcé. My ex-wife, Tiffany, and I were married five years, and I've been divorced just as long. Since Tiffany, I've dated, but never gotten serious about anyone."

"No law says you have to. Nothing wrong with dating for fun."

"I know that. My parents are just overeager for grandchildren. Hadley marrying Devon took some of the heat off me and Savion. Still, they think I'm a playboy because I haven't come home with a fiancée yet."

Her eyes narrowed slightly, not in a menacing way, but as if she were analyzing his words. "Are they right?"

"No." He held her gaze. "I haven't gotten serious about anyone because I haven't really connected with anyone."

Her lips bowed as if she was going to say something. But she remained silent.

The conversation they'd had still hung in the back of his mind, and he was still frustrated with her. Yet there was no denying the way he felt whenever he was in her presence. Knowing full well he might regret it later, he reached over the center console to take her hand in his. "I hadn't connected with anyone…until you."

Her eyes widened. "Campbell, I…"

"You don't have to say anything. You were right earlier. You don't owe me anything." He gave her hand a gentle squeeze. "But we both know there's something between us. And you owe it to yourself to see where it could lead."

Her eyelids fluttered in a succession of rapid blinks. "I…I…"

He released her hand. "Do you want me to walk you to the door?"

She shook her head.

He got out, walked around to her side and opened the door for her. "Have a good day, Sierra."

"You, too." She unbuckled her seat belt, climbed out of his car and took several brisk steps away.

Smiling, he shut the door and got back in on the driver's side.

When he looked up again, he saw her standing on the landing, leaning against the railing.

And as he pulled away, his last view of her was of her watching him, with the wind swirling her hair around her beautiful face like a shimmering halo.

Chapter 7

Seated on the small stool by the vanity in her dressing room Friday, Sierra leaned closer to the mirror, so she could see what she was doing. With the cleansing towelette, she wiped away the last visible traces of the heavy makeup she'd been wearing all morning. She loved a glamorous look, but wasn't particularly fond of the makeup she wore on-screen. When shooting ended, she would immediately grab for her package of makeup wipes.

Outside the door, the rest of the studio remained alive with activity, despite the wrapping of the day's shooting. She could hear the footsteps and conversations of people walking up and down the corridor as she brushed her hair up and away from her face.

She'd just grabbed an elastic and looped it around her hair when someone knocked on the door. Securing the ponytail as she walked, she pulled the door open.

"I see you've taken your face off," Jazmin quipped as she entered the room.

Sierra laughed. "Don't I always? You know I'm ready to drop the mask as soon as the director says it's a wrap."

Flopping down on the black love seat, Jazmin crossed her legs and sat back. "Listen. We gotta talk…"

Before Jazmin could finish her sentence, Mia appeared in the open doorway. "What's up, senior citizens?"

Sierra rolled her eyes. "How are you, Mia?"

"I'm just grand, thank you. Despite what people may say, I'm always on top of my game." Mia braced her shoulder against the door frame, crossing her narrow arms over her chest. "That's never going to change, ma'am."

"Good to know." Sierra's flat tone conveyed her general disinterest in Mia's foolishness.

"Well, I won't stay too long. I know you old ladies need your naps." Straightening up, Mia executed a dramatic turn, placed a hand on her hip and strutted away.

Sierra looked to her friend. "What the hell was that?"

Jazmin shook her head. "Shenanigans. That's why

I came in here to talk to you. I knew she was gonna be on the warpath."

Taking a seat next to her friend, Sierra asked, "What bug is up her butt now?"

Reaching into her large black purse, Jazmin pulled out her phone. "I know you don't read reviews, but you need to know what's being said about the show."

She shook her head. "No, Jazzy. You know why I don't read reviews. It just makes me anxious. I gave up reading them years ago, and it's the best decision I ever made. Avoiding them keeps my sanity intact."

"Trust me, I get it." Jazmin scrolled through something on her phone's screen. "Still, you need to hear this, so just listen."

Resting her hands in her lap, she tucked her feet beneath her bottom and braced herself for what she was about to hear. "Okay. I'm listening."

Jazmin cleared her throat. "'Television's new hit drama, *The Shores*, follows a group of friends and their glamorous life in a luxurious small town. Set and filmed on a small island just off the North Carolina coast, the show delivers great scenery, compelling dialogue and storylines that rival the old nighttime soaps like *Dynasty* and *Knot's Landing*.'"

Sierra exhaled. "All good, so far."

Jazmin put up her hand. "There's more." She scrolled again. "'Viewers looking for soapy goodness will love the show, especially the sharp-tongued diva Karen Drake, played expertly by actress Sierra Dandridge. Dandridge's performance has drawn raves from critics of every stripe, and for good reason: she's brilliant in the role.'"

Sierra felt her cheeks warm. "That's great to hear, but I'm not seeing the problem yet…"

Jazmin read further. "'In contrast to Dandridge's stellar turn as Drake, young model-turned-actress Mia Leigh's performance as lead character Fiona LaSalle is lackluster at best. It seems Ms. Leigh has brought the flat, expressionless face we often see on high-fashion runways into her acting, and it detracts tremendously from her scenes.'"

Sucking in a breath through her clenched teeth, Sierra shook her head. "Well, damn."

Jazmin turned off the screen and put the phone back in her bag. "Now you know what the problem is between you two."

Sierra pressed her fingers to her temple. "Oh, come on. That reviewer was a little harsh, yes. But it's only one review."

Jazmin shook her head, lips pursed. "If only, boo. If you read the reviews, you'd know they're all like that."

Her eyes widened. "Really?"

Jazmin nodded. "Yes, really. My intern pulls all the reviews for me, and I've seen at least twenty. Only one of those had anything favorable to say about Mia, and that was all about how good she looked on-screen."

"You're telling me all the critics are praising my performance, and panning Mia's?"

"That's exactly what I'm telling you." Jazmin stifled a yawn. "So now you know why Mia's been acting the way she has with you."

Sierra sighed. "There's the last piece of that puzzle." She'd noticed how Mia didn't seem to have any problems with the other cast or crew members, only her. *Now it makes sense, but what can I do about it?* "There doesn't seem to be a good way to fix this. I can't change what the critics have already said. What am I supposed to do, give a crappy performance to make her look better by comparison?"

Jazmin chuckled. "Mia is just petty enough that she'd probably love that."

Sierra rolled her eyes.

"But we both know you're not going to do it. Sierra Dandridge doesn't roll like that."

"Damn straight." She looked toward her vanity, wondering how to handle this situation. "Any suggestions? What do you think I should do?"

With a shrug, Jazmin stood. "I don't think you have to do anything, really. If Mia keeps doing what she's doing, it's going to catch up with her eventually."

"I don't know." Sierra didn't know how much more of Mia's crap she could put up with before she decked the girl.

"Think about it. The critics all think her acting is terrible, and she's been a total brat to you on set. Meanwhile you're getting all the starred reviews and accolades." She slung the purse strap over her shoulder. "The way I see it, all you have to do is be patient, and remain professional. Let Ms. Leigh keep right on digging her own grave, and you'll come out on top once she's buried herself in the dirt."

Sierra nodded. "Makes sense, I guess."

"Of course it does." Jazmin winked. "I'm going home. I'm beat. Later, girl."

Sierra waved as Jazmin slipped out. Alone again in the quiet dressing room, she thought about what her friend had said.

Be patient and remain professional. She'd been doing it all this time; she supposed it wouldn't be too hard to keep it up.

She went around the room, tidying up and tossing things into her bag. Then she grabbed the bag by the handles, turned off the lights and locked up her dressing room.

In the studio parking lot, she opened the passenger side door of her rental and tossed the bag in. When she shut the door, she looked up and saw Mia standing on the sidewalk several yards away, talking to someone.

Mia cut her eyes at Sierra, her stare venomous.

Sierra pretended to ignore her, climbing into the car and driving away.

As she drove toward the condo, her mind drifted to Campbell. She thought about sitting in his convertible, feeling the warmth of his hand wrapped around hers. She remembered what he'd said to her yesterday, about how he hadn't connected with an-

other woman the way he had with her. *Was he being
sincere? Or was he just sweet-talking me?* Her ide-
alistic side wanted to believe what he'd said. Her
cynical side reminded her that even if he were honest (and he probably wasn't), it wouldn't matter. She
didn't have time to date right now. Things at work
were way too complicated for her to add a relationship to the mix.

She sighed. When it came to romance, the timing
just never seemed to be right.

It was just after two when Campbell finally took
his lunch break, and as he entered the break room
with his take-out wings and fries from the Salty
Siren, he saw his brother and sister were in the room,
as well.

"Hey, Cam." Hadley, seated on the far side of the
table, smiled at her phone screen as she spoke.

"Hey, sis. Savion." Campbell sat down across
from his sister, setting his food on the table in front
of him. Then he took the folder of paperwork he'd
had tucked beneath his arm, and laid that down, as
well, a safe distance from the food. His workload
necessitated bringing the paperwork in here, but he
didn't want to smudge or damage it.

Savion, sitting in a chair he'd pulled over to the
countertop, waved. Then he returned his attention
to the black, leather-bound day planner he carried
with him everywhere, scrawling something in its
pages with a pen.

Campbell frowned as he looked at his brother. "What are you working on, bro?"

Savion shook his head and raised his gaze from the pages. "Nothing."

Campbell didn't believe that for a second. His brother took that planner everywhere with him. Hell, he probably took it with him to the bathroom. *What is he writing in that thing, anyhow?* Despite his curiosity, he knew Savion wouldn't answer any follow-up questions, so he didn't bother asking any.

While Campbell unwrapped his food, Hadley sat across from him, smiling and giggling at her phone. She would type something, then a few seconds later her phone would buzz, and she'd read the screen and giggle again. He could only assume she was texting back and forth with someone.

Looking between the two of them, he said, "There are three people in here. Only one of us is eating. What are y'all doing in here, anyway?"

"Coffee break." Savion gestured toward his ceramic mug sitting on the counter next to him.

"Same." Hadley ran her thumb over her screen. "I already had my coffee, but I'm texting with Devon."

Campbell simply shook his head and turned his attention back to his food. After all this time of being called out as the "lazy" one, he found it hilarious that he was the only one in there who'd brought work with him. He supposed it was possible Savion was working, since Campbell couldn't see what he was writing, but the odds of that seemed pretty slim.

They should be at their desks if they aren't going to be eating.

It didn't take long for him to get his fill of their sitting around, lollygagging. "You know, you two are always giving me flak about not doing enough work." He gestured to the open folder on the table next to him. "Looks like today I'm the only one interested in getting anything accomplished."

Savion rolled his eyes.

Hadley pursed her lips. "Ease up, Campbell. I'm just messaging my husband for a minute."

"Nah. You've been sitting here for a good while, Hadley. You already had your coffee, you said that yourself." He popped a fry into his mouth, chewed and swallowed. "And you, Savion. For all we know you could be drawing stick figures in your planner. Both of you should be in your offices."

He scoffed. "I'm the eldest, and the senior executive in this office. So you can quit making demands anytime, lil bro." Savion stood, flipped his planner shut, and then he and his coffee cup vacated the room.

Campbell turned his attention back to Hadley. "Sis, you're the reasonable one in the office."

She looked up from her phone, smiled in his direction. "So, you finally admit it?"

He waved his hand. "Don't get too excited or I'll never admit it again. Anyway, you have to have noticed how hard I've been working lately."

She tipped her head to one side, then nodded.

"I've noticed, Cam. I know you've been doing more around here, and I'm proud of you."

"Thanks. It's nice to know someone here sees my efforts." He dipped one of his oven-roasted wings into a cup of ranch dressing. "You've been working way less hours since you got married."

She winked. "I can't leave my husband to fend for himself. Gotta handle my wifely duties."

Campbell gave her a sideways glance. "Please, don't elaborate."

She stood then, punching him playfully in the shoulder as she passed. "Don't hate, Cam. Anyway, let me get back to work." Pocketing her phone, she strolled out of the break room.

For the next twenty minutes, he alternated between eating and reading the paperwork, careful not to smudge it.

He tried to focus on the words on the forms, but found his mind wandering. Visions of Sierra's beautiful face kept appearing in his mind. If someone had told him a year ago that he'd have spent a night in the home of his favorite actress, he would never have believed it. And yet now that he'd experienced spending time with Sierra, he couldn't seem to stop thinking about her.

Good sense told him to walk away, to keep his distance from her. But he'd never been very good at exercising good sense, not where women were involved. His heart, foolish though it may be, told him to pursue her. This went beyond the schoolboy crush

he'd had on her when she'd been a beautiful, yet un-
attainable fantasy. She was literally close enough
to touch now, and he wanted more. He wanted to
get to know who she really was beneath the mask,
beneath the protective layers of dismissiveness she
wore like a suit of winter gear. Who was the real Sierra Dandridge? He had to know. His curiosity demanded satisfaction.

Tossing his empty food containers in the trash,
Campbell grabbed his paperwork and went back to
his own office to finish.

Alone in his office, he set about his work. The
rote motions of filling in the forms allowed his mind
to wander, and this time, he found himself thinking
back on his relationship with Tiffany, his ex. He'd
given her his name, a comfortable home and five
years of his life. He'd been faithful to her and done
his best to make her happy. He'd loved her, or at least
the version of her he knew. Tiffany had been a career
go-getter from the start of their relationship, and it
was one of the reasons he loved her. He found her
drive to succeed inspiring.

That was, until he discovered just why she'd been
pulling all those extra hours, and it hadn't been to
move up the career ladder.

He thought back to that fateful conversation. It
had been shortly before their fifth anniversary, and
they'd been talking about their future. He'd wanted
to talk about starting a family, but she'd been reluc-
tant. Finally, after he pressed her, she'd admitted

that she'd been seeing a man she worked with for the previous two years.

He'd been stunned and wounded to hear her words, so casually tossed out in the middle of a conversation. He knew then that he could never stay with someone so duplicitous, who'd lied to his face all that time. Four days later, just after their anniversary, he'd filed for divorce.

He sighed, pushing the thoughts away. Logic told him to forget about Tiffany, and to remember that not all women were like her.

But his heart, wary of bearing such pain ever again, told him something else.

He had to protect himself, no matter the cost.

Chapter 8

Saturday morning, Sierra sat at a small table inside of The Heavenly Bean. The cute little coffee shop was in the heart of the downtown district and served a fantastic café mocha. Her seat by the window allowed her a great view of everything happening outside, so as she sipped from her mug, she let her eyes scan the scenery.

She'd agreed to meet Jazmin here for a quick breakfast, but as usual, her friend was running late. As the moments ticked by, Sierra found herself thinking about Campbell...again. It seemed he was always on her mind. Every moment she wasn't actively occupied with something, thoughts of him rose.

Enough of this. She put down her mug and picked

up her phone. Searching through her call list, she dialed the number Campbell had called her from a few days prior.

He answered after the second ring. "Hello?"

"Campbell, hi. It's Sierra."

"Good morning. How are you?" He sounded calm and pleased to hear from her.

Hearing his voice made her smile. "I'm fine, thanks. How are you?"

"Good." He paused, his tone changing to concern. "Is there a problem at the condo? Something you need fixed?"

"No, no. Everything's fine there."

"Glad to hear that." He seemed relieved. "Although now I'm really curious about why you called me."

She drew a deep breath. "Listen, I don't want to waste your time. Do you think we could maybe get together and talk? Just the two of us?"

After a few silent beats, he spoke again. "Are you asking me out on a date?"

A tingle of discomfort crawled up her neck, and her eyes darted around the coffee shop as she answered. "No, no. It's definitely not a date. I just think we need to talk about some things. You know, come to an understanding."

"About what?"

She cleared her throat, keeping her voice low. "About what happened at the condo the other night.

And about what you said to me in your car, when you dropped me off."

"I agree. We do need to talk, about both of those things. When do you want to have this conversation?"

"Are you busy later this afternoon?"

"That's kind of short notice," he teased. "But lucky for you, I'm free. So, what do you have in mind?"

She thought for a moment. She didn't want to take him back to the condo, because that seemed too intimate. The same went for asking to meet at his place. *We need to meet somewhere neutral, somewhere public.* She snapped her fingers as the idea came to her. "Why don't we meet on the beach? I'll bring the food if you bring something to drink and that plaid blanket."

"I can agree to that. Although, you have to admit, this sounds a lot like a romantic evening." He made a soft whistling sound. "You know, just the two of us on the beach, with wine and a big blanket…"

She cleared her throat. "Excuse me, who said anything about wine? You can just bring some sodas or bottled water, thank you very much."

His low, easy laugh followed her words. "You're just determined not to have any fun."

She scoffed. "That's not it. I just want to make sure you understand what this is."

"And what is it?"

She shifted in her seat, searching for just the right

descriptive phrase. "It's a casual picnic between friends."

He laughed again. "If you say so."

She rolled her eyes, unable to decide if she was more amused or annoyed with him. If she couldn't control the direction of this conversation, how was she going to control the direction of things once she met with him? "So are you agreeing?"

"Sure. We can go out."

"Campbell, it's not a date." The moment the words left Sierra's lips, she glanced up to see Jazmin approaching the table. When she sat in the chair across from her, her friend's wide-eyed, openmouthed stare told her she'd heard Sierra's exclamation. *Awesome.*

"Yes, I remember." Campbell's voice drew her out of her embarrassment and back into their conversation. "How does five thirty at Richardson Point Pier sound for our 'not-a-date'?"

She turned away from Jazmin's scrutiny to hide her smile. "Sounds great. See you there."

"Later, Sierra." He disconnected the call.

She laid her phone facedown on the table, then went fishing in her purse. She didn't need anything out of her bag. She just needed a reason to avoid Jazmin's questioning gaze.

Jazmin cleared her throat. "Girl, if you don't quit pretending to look for something in your bag and look at me, I'm coming around this table."

Shaking her head, she set her purse aside and looked her friend in the eyes. "Okay. Go ahead."

"Did I just hear you say you're going out with Campbell?" Her expression held a mixture of curiosity and humor.

"Yes, nosy. But just like I told him, it's not a date."

"Whatever, girl. Call it whatever you want, but you could definitely use some male company in your life." She picked up the laminated menu resting in the iron holder on the table.

"Oh, quit, Jazmin. You act like I haven't been on a date in the last decade or something."

Jazmin fixed her with a pointed gaze. "Sierra, when was the last time you went on a date? Better yet, when was the last time you got some?"

Sierra pursed her lips. "Shh! We're in public. Don't talk so loud."

Jazmin folded her arms over her chest. "That long, huh?"

"It's only been about five months." She grabbed her own menu and looked over it, even though she already knew what she wanted.

Jazmin's next words fell out in a harsh whisper. "You haven't gotten any in five months?"

"That was my last date. The last time I got busy was probably six months ago."

This time Jazmin didn't say anything. She just gave a series of slow, rather dramatic blinks.

Sierra rolled her eyes. "It doesn't matter. Like I said, this is…"

"Yeah, yeah. It's not a date." Jazmin shook her head. "Let me ask you this. The last time you made love. Was it good enough to last you the rest of your life?"

"Nah." She remembered the encounter with her ex-boyfriend, but not because it was spectacularly good. His lack of concern for her pleasure was what led to the demise of their brief relationship. Since then, it had just seemed like less trouble to put those thoughts out of her mind. And she'd succeeded at doing that…until Campbell entered her space.

"I'm not trying to define what you're doing with Campbell. And you don't have to, either." Her friend set the menu down, apparently decided on what she would order. "All I'm saying is, if he offers you the good stuff, consider taking him up on it."

Blowing out a breath, Sierra sipped from her now tepid mocha. "Let's just order. I'm starved."

They went to the counter and put in their orders. Each item on the breakfast menu took its name from one of the lighthouses dotting the North Carolina coastline, a few of which were visible from Sapphire Shores. Sierra requested the Cape Hatteras: egg white, spinach and white cheddar on brioche, while Jazmin went for the Okracoke, bacon, egg and sharp cheddar on a croissant.

Back at the table with their food, they dug in.

Swallowing a mouthful, Jazmin remarked, "You know I only tease you out of love, right?"

She smiled. "Yes, Jazzy. I know."

"I just want you to be happy."

"You're happy, and you don't have a man."

"Trust me, girl. It ain't from lack of trying."

Sierra's burst of laughter turned quite a few heads in the coffee shop. Jazmin added a much-needed levity to her life, as well as a practical perspective. Jazmin had been the one to convince her to accept the role on the show and come to the island in the first place. They'd been friends for almost a decade and had navigated their fair share of the craziness that characterized life as women of color in the film industry. "I love you right back. Even though you get on my last nerve sometimes."

"That's what friends are for." Jazmin winked.

Shaking her head, Sierra put her focus back on her breakfast.

Still, she couldn't help thinking about what Jazmin had said. What would happen on this "not-a-date"? Would it go the way she planned? Or would Campbell's charm overwhelm her?

Guess there's only one way to find out.

Campbell arrived at Richardson Point Pier around a quarter after five. He'd wanted to get there a bit early on purpose, so he could stake out a good spot on the strip of beach. The sun still sat high in the sky, and there was plenty of daylight left. The perfect setting for his "not-a-date" with Sierra.

There were a few benches installed among the dunes, set back about a half mile from the water. He spread out his trusty plaid blanket on the sand several steps from one of the benches. From his canvas grocery bag, he pulled out the chilled bottle and the plastic flutes. Once he'd placed the bottle in the small bucket and surrounded it with gel ice cubes, he sat down on the blanket to admire the scenery and get himself together before Sierra arrived.

He faced the water, letting his eyes sweep over the rippling blue surface toward the horizon. A few gulls circled overhead, calling to each other and intermittently swooping down in search of a fish or two. The rich blue sky held only a few thin, wispy clouds, and the air on his skin felt warm and comforting, like an embrace. The day was so nice, it was hard to believe a tropical storm had passed only a few days ago. He wasn't the only one taking advantage of the weather, and he spent the next few minutes people watching. There were families out, young children splashing in the water or building sandcastles. Couples strolled along the water's edge, holding hands. There were a few folks out being active, running or walking their dogs. He even saw a lone guy in a baseball cap and shorts, using his metal detector to comb the beach for hidden treasures.

As an angsty teen, in the throes of his middle-child blues, he'd often come here and sat on a bench for hours, watching his neighbors moving up and down the beach. Somehow it had made him feel less lonely, less left out. He didn't have as much time on his hands now as he did back then, but he liked to come here as often as he could. These people, out walking, running and enjoying the beach, were the threads that wove together to make the island such a wonderful place to live. There had been times in the past when he'd thought of leaving and seeking his fortune elsewhere. The older he got, though, the more he felt connected to the island. Now he didn't know if he'd ever live anywhere else.

The wind changed direction, and he picked up the familiar scent of her: the citrus and cinnamon combination that had ruled his mind that night in the condo. Turning at the waist, he saw her strolling over the sand toward him.

She wore a knee-length white sundress that bared her arms and legs to the sun, as well as a pair of flesh-colored sandals embellished with crystals. She'd tucked her hair up on top of her head in a neat bun, and wore no jewelry except for a pair of diamond studs sparkling in her ears. Her eyes were hidden away behind a pair of gold-rimmed sunglasses with rose-tinted lenses. The handle of an oval-shaped basket rested in the crook of her elbow. She smiled in his direction.

He smiled back. She looked radiant, fresh and, best of all, happy to see him.

"Hi, Campbell." She gave a little wave.

"Hey, Sierra." He stood as she reached the blanket. "Here, I'll take that." He grabbed the basket by the handle and set it down on the blanket. "It's heavy. You must have brought something really good."

She knelt on the blanket next to the basket. "I whipped up some pasta primavera and grilled chicken. And sugar cookies for dessert. How does that sound?"

He made a show of rubbing his stomach as he joined her on the blanket. "Sounds like the best non-date I've ever been on."

She giggled, jabbing him playfully with her elbow. Gesturing to his small galvanized bucket, she said, "What's that? I thought you were bringing soda?"

He shrugged. "You were the one who suggested soda. I'm not a big soda drinker, so I decided to just bring a little bubbly instead."

She pursed her lips. "Campbell, you know I'm not about to sit out here and drink alcohol with you. We're not on a date, remember?"

He shook his head. "I know what this is…and what it isn't." He reached into the bucket and lifted the bottle, so she could read the label. "But what's a little sparkling grape juice between friends?"

She threw her head back and laughed.

The musical sound of her amusement touched his heart. She struck him as driven, focused and super serious. Knowing that he could get her to let go of that rigidity made him feel good in a way he hadn't expected.

When she finally got the giggles under control, she shook her head. "Oh, goodness. You are such a mess."

"I'll keep it up all day if it makes you laugh like that." He winked.

That set her to laughing again. He enjoyed seeing her this way, so lighthearted.

When the second round of laughter ended, she pulled out the hand sanitizer. With both their hands properly cleaned, she started pulling out the spread: plastic plates and utensils, and the container holding the still-warm pasta. She took off the lid, releasing the fragrant aroma into the air, and served them each a generous portion.

While they ate, they chatted and watched the rolling waves.

With their empty plates back in the basket, she sat next to him, her legs stretched in front of her and crossed at the ankles. Between nibbles of a sugar cookie, she talked about her childhood. "My parents gave me possibly the most straitlaced, dull upbringing possible. We lived in the burbs, far from all the excitement in Los Angeles. I took ballet, learned to play the cello, studied Mandarin Chinese."

"Sounds like you had a lot of great experiences," he remarked. "Your parents wanted to expose you to the arts, culture and foreign languages."

"I know. I appreciate everything they did for me. They also put a lot of pressure on me. It was always 'Sierra, be responsible.' Or 'Sierra, study hard.' I love them so much, but I couldn't wait to graduate and get out of there."

He listened to her words and heard the undertones. From the way she described her youth, it became clearer to him how she'd developed her serious outlook.

"They weren't terribly excited about me pursuing an acting career, either." She finished her cookie, then took a long sip from her flute. "They eventually came around, though."

"Our relationships with our parents can be really complicated," Cam mused. "When we were kids, my siblings and I knew we'd better do as we were told or catch all hell. Nowadays, we still love and respect Mom and Dad, but there's also an element of friendship between us."

"I think the change happens when our parents start to see us as adults." She set down her empty flute, then lifted the shades from her eyes. Her gaze resting on the water, she sighed. "I don't think that happened with my parents until I was well into my twenties."

He chuckled. "Same here. My mom used to follow me around with a lint roller. She was always fixing my clothes, trying to tie my ties, all of that. She kept it up until I was about twenty-six."

Sierra laughed again. "I think that's kind of sweet."

"Yeah, but try explaining to your date why your mama's brushing your hair."

Grinning, she admitted, "I can see how that would be awkward."

"It put a hell of a damper on my dating life. One woman called me a 'mama's boy.'"

She reached over, gave his hand a little squeeze. "If it makes you feel any better, I see you as a full-grown man."

Their gazes met and locked.

"I gotta tell you, that does make me feel better. A lot better."

They remained that way, lost in each other's eyes, for several long moments. His lips tingled with the desire to kiss her, but he held back. She'd been very clear about this from the beginning. It wasn't a date. *I'm not going to pressure her.*

He set aside his wants in favor of her comfort. The evening would progress on her terms.

If any kissing happened between them, she'd have to be the one to initiate it.

Chapter 9

Sierra released a contented sigh as she sat next to Campbell, watching the sun set. The last time she'd taken the time to sit and watch the event from start to finish had been years ago, back in film school. Back then, she'd been out carousing with her classmates by a bonfire. She could remember the excitement of that night, the feeling of freedom.

Yet, sitting here with him, she felt something else. She felt calm, as if she were meant to be in his company. Being here with him felt as natural as the celestial event happening above them.

She glanced his way. His eyes were on the horizon, taking in the spectacular beauty of nature. She watched the shadows playing over his face, and she realized she wanted to know him. She'd told him a bit of her life story, and now she wanted to hear some of his.

As the darkness set in, and many of the other beachgoers packed up and left, she shifted closer to him.

He turned to her, offering a grin, but saying nothing as she cozied up to his side. The heat of his body curled around her as their thighs brushed against each other. To keep from reaching for him, she laced her fingers together.

She felt the spark between them, and she knew that, without a distraction, this "not-a-date" would soon take a very date-like turn. She scooted away from him, climbing to her feet. "I'm still feeling kind of full from dinner. Would you mind taking a walk with me?"

"I'm game." He took off his leather sandals and placed them on the blanket. Then he stood, towering over her once he got on his feet.

She kicked off her jeweled slides, leaving them next to his shoes. They started walking toward the pier, moving close to the water's edge. She thrilled at the cool liquid lapping around her ankles as they strolled down the sandy strip. She tried to walk next to him, but remained a step or two behind because his legs were so much longer than hers.

"Thanks for walking with me."

"No problem."

"Tell me your story. What was it like growing up around here?"

He hummed low in his throat, as if thinking about what to say. "Well, the major thing I remember is feeling like everybody here knew everybody else. I don't think it's just Sapphire Shores, I think it's probably like that in every small town. I guess it's a little more intense here because we're separated from the folks on the mainland."

She nodded. "I can see that. Even in the few weeks I've been here, I've picked up on that. This is a very neighborly place."

"Right. That meant I couldn't cut up as a young-ster." He slowed his steps, as if he'd noticed her struggle to keep up. "My parents basically had a network of spies and informants. Wherever I went, if I acted the fool, they would know about it before I got home."

She couldn't help laughing, at both his statement and his tone. "Sorry, but it sounds funny when you say it that way. What were things like at home, with your brother and sister?" As an only child, she'd often wondered what it would have been like to have a sibling.

"Savion's the oldest and the most serious. He's al-ways been that way. Even when we were kids he was always trying to supervise us. Hadley's the baby, and she's a little bit spoiled. She's grown up to be very capable and independent, though."

Sierra could tell he loved both his siblings, but he

seemed especially proud of his sister. "What about you, Campbell? What were you like as a kid?"

He shrugged. "I kind of did my own thing. I grew up being the only one in the house who liked comic books. I was pretty active, too. Skateboarding, surfing, played baseball in high school."

She was impressed. *Now I know why he's got the athletic body type.* "Do you still do any of those things?"

"I still read comic books." He chuckled. "You couldn't pay me to get on a skateboard these days. But I do play the occasional game of baseball. Every other year I play in a property managers association game for charity."

Hearing all this about his life satisfied one side of her curiosity, and piqued the other. She wasn't sure how he'd react to her next question, but knew she had to ask it anyway. "I hope you don't mind me asking, but can you tell me a little about your marriage?"

He stopped walking, turned to look at her. "Really? Why?"

She looked away from his piercing eyes, toward the dark surface of the water. "I'm curious. I can't really explain why. We're learning about each other, and I know your ex-wife was a part of your life. Past relationships are part of what makes us who we are."

He released a long breath through his lips. "Her name is Tiffany. I loved her, and I believe she loved me. Being married to her was like being married to two different people."

Sierra frowned. "How so?"

"In public, she came across as very confident and capable. In private, however, she was fragile, unsure of herself and clingy." He started rubbing his hands together. "She couldn't understand why I wanted time alone, to pursue my own interests. And when she decided she wanted more attention than I could give her, she sought that attention elsewhere."

Seeing the expression on his face, and the way he kept rubbing his hands, Sierra touched his shoulder. "I'm sorry, Campbell. I didn't mean to upset you."

He stopped fidgeting, stuffing his hands into the pockets of his shorts. "It's okay. I'm fine."

She didn't think he was fine. Still, she knew pressing the issue would get her nowhere. She couldn't imagine how painful it must have been for him to discover his ex-wife's infidelity. So rather than make him relive it any longer, she changed the subject. "Something else I wanted to ask. Have you ever lived anywhere else?"

"Just in college. I got my bachelor's in hospitality and tourism administration from NC Central, so I lived in Durham for those four years. Other than that, I've pretty much only lived here. I've traveled a lot, but I've never made my home anywhere else." He started walking again.

She followed him, catching up more easily this time. "Have you ever wanted to live somewhere else?"

"Not really. There's something special about the island, something I don't think I can find anywhere else." He turned and started walking back the way they'd come.

"We're turning back?"

"We have to. Beyond that sign up there is private property." He gestured to a blue metal sign nearby.

She nodded, following him. This time, rather than chase him, she caught hold of his hand.

He looked back at her, appearing surprised for a moment. But he held her hand anyway, and a smile touched her lips.

As they neared the pier again, he led her underneath it. There, he leaned his back against one of the supportive wooden columns. Clasping both her hands, he said, "Sierra, I've got to say something, and I don't know if you're going to like it."

She braced for whatever would come next. "What is it?"

"I know what you've been saying all day, but this is starting to feel dangerously like a date." He stared down into her eyes.

Gazing up at him, she nodded. "You're right." Taking a step closer to him, she raised her hand and stroked her open palm along his jawline. "And as it turns out, I'm okay with that."

He smiled. "Good. Because I don't think there's any way we can stop what's happening between us."

"I don't think I want to stop it anymore, Campbell." She leaned in, raising her face to him.

A moment later, his lips met hers, and the whole world melted away. His strong arms circled her waist, while she tossed her arms around his shoulders. Her mouth opened and their tongues mated. She could taste the remnants of sweetness left behind by the grape juice. His kissing, skillful and passionate, had her seeing stars. She never wanted this to end, never wanted him to let her go. The heat of his body combined with the potency of his kiss made her feel alive in a way she never had before.

When he broke the kiss, she took a moment to catch her breath. Still in his arms, she whispered in his ear, "Spend the night with me, Campbell."

He touched her cheek. "Are you sure that's what you want?"

"It isn't what I want." She kissed his fingertips. "It's what I need."

Campbell swore the drive back to Sierra's condo was the longest he'd ever taken. After her whispered invitation, they'd dashed across the sand to gather their things, then gotten into their cars to go to her place. He couldn't remember the last time he'd struggled so much to focus. Her touch, the look in her eyes and the way she'd asked him to come home with her had him so turned on he wasn't sure he'd remember how to get there if not for following her car.

When they finally made it to the house, he kept pace with her as she ran up the stairs. Inside the condo, she locked them inside and tossed her keys in the bowl on the table near the door. He dragged her against his body and captured her lips again.

He kissed her with all the hunger he felt inside, working his hands into her hair. The bun came loose, and her hair fell free beneath his fingertips as the kiss deepened. Her legs began to tremble, and without breaking the kiss, he turned her and braced her against the closed door.

Between their bodies, his hardness grew and throbbed. He wanted her with every cell in his body. He moved one of his hands down the right side of her body, dragging it down to the hem of her dress and then slipping it underneath. When he cupped her bottom, and gave it a gentle squeeze, she released a soft moan into his mouth.

The sound pushed him to the edge of his self-control. Breaking the kiss, he looked into her eyes. "We need to move this party to the bedroom, before I take you against the door."

A wicked gleam lit her eyes.

He grabbed her hand and led her down the hallway to the master bedroom.

There, he watched as she stood by the bed, facing him. She stepped out of her shoes and kicked them aside. Grasping the hem of her dress, she pulled it up over her head and tossed it aside. His eyes widened at the sight of her soft blue lace bra and panties. He kicked off his sandals for the second time tonight and closed the distance between them.

He splayed his palm over the flat plane of her stomach. "You're so beautiful."

She gave him a naughty little smile. "You haven't even seen it all yet."

He growled low in his throat. Snatching off his own T-shirt and shorts, he tossed the clothing to the floor. Gently, he guided her back until she lay horizontally across the bed.

With a slow, deliberate hand, he caressed each inch of bared skin. He stroked lazy fingers over her shoulders, then cupped the mounds of her breasts. Her arms, her stomach, her long, shapely legs…he left no part untouched. By the time he reached beneath her to undo her bra, her rapid breathing turned to a soft sigh. He worked the clasps free as she leaned up to his kiss, then freed her from the bra. He took her panties from her and added them to the growing pile on the floor.

Her nudity overwhelmed him. She was more beautiful than he could have ever imagined. The womanly curves of her body were as lush as the rain forest, and twice as breathtaking. His manhood pulsed with need for her, but he restrained himself. She might not be a novice at lovemaking, but it was still their first time together. He wanted to bring her to the heights of passion in a slow, languid fashion that assured him she would never forget this night, no matter what happened in the future.

Stripping off his boxers, he rejoined her on the bed and drew her into his arms. He kissed her lips, her jawline, the hollow of her neck. He flicked his tongue over her collarbone, then took his time suckling at each dark nipple until she cried out.

"Campbell." Her words were a faint whisper in the dark. "Please."

He heard the pleading in her tone, and knew it was time. He left her for only a moment, to sheath himself with protection, before returning to her. Adjusting himself so that he knelt between her parted thighs, he caressed her hips with his palms. "I know, honey. Let me fix it."

A heartbeat later he pressed himself against her opening. She was slick with desire, and as he pushed inside, her tight warmth enticed him to go as deep as possible. She purred as he entered her fully and rocked his hips.

She soon joined in the rhythm, her hips rising to meet his every stroke. He gritted his teeth, keeping a tenuous hold on his self-control as her body enveloped him with magnificent heat.

She clung to him, her throaty sighs coming in time with his thrusts. He caught a glimpse of her, head thrown back, spine arched like a drawn bow, as she screamed her completion. Seeing her go over the edge pushed him over, as well, and he pulled her close and growled his release into the crown of her hair.

Later, in the silence, he lay awake with her in his arms. He listened to her soft breathing, and felt his heart turn over in his chest. With her naked body fitted against his, she seemed so content. Her sleeping face, so peaceful in the moonlight, reflected the peace he felt inside.

He remembered the days when he would enjoy a woman's company, then return home directly afterward. But with Sierra, something shifted inside him, something he couldn't name. He didn't want to let her go, didn't want to leave her warmth behind to seek his own bed. So instead of trying to extricate himself from her while she slept, he grabbed the covers and pulled them up over their bodies.

Chapter 10

Sunday morning, Sierra awakened alone in her bed. She sat upright, searching through sleep-heavy eyes for any sign of Campbell. She didn't see anything, but she did smell something delicious coming from the kitchen. A smile touched her lips. *He's in there cooking.*

She lay back against the pillows for a moment, letting the erotic memories of the night before wash over her. She could still feel the light throbbing between her thighs, reminding her of the way he'd loved her well into the night. There had been no man before him who had given her that kind of pleasure, and in her heart, she knew no other man would be able to live up to him.

Feeling the emotions rise within her, she did her best to tamp them down. What they'd done last night had been the culmination of their undeniable attraction to each other. It didn't mean they were in a relationship. Or did it?

Not wanting to dwell on that, she got out of bed and entered the master bathroom. She stepped into the stream of hot water, cleansing her body of the sweat she'd worked up last night. Freshly washed, she emerged from the bathroom and slipped into a clean cotton tee that grazed her knees.

She was sitting on the edge of the bed putting on lotion when he entered the room, a tray in hand. He'd put his shorts back on, but had forgone a shirt, leaving the hard, muscled lines of his chest bared to her appreciative gaze.

"Good morning, sleepyhead." He sat the tray on the bed and leaned down to kiss her forehead. "Are you hungry?"

She nodded. "This looks and smells fantastic." There were two plates on the tray, holding scrambled eggs, wheat toast, strips of turkey bacon and mounds of grits running with butter. There were also two glasses of ice-cold cranberry juice. "You're really trying to spoil me."

He smiled. "Just a little something I threw together. Go ahead, dig in."

She stood. "As soon as I wash my hands, I will." When she got back from taking care of that, she sat cross-legged on the bed and picked up her fork and plate. Resting the plate in her lap, she forked up some of the grits. They were just as delicious as they looked, and so was the rest of the food.

While they ate, he grabbed the remote from the nightstand and turned on the wall-mounted flat screen. The picture came on, and he flipped a few channels before stopping. "Looks like they're playing a rerun of *The Shores.*"

She looked up, and sure enough, her face was on the screen. She washed down a mouthful of food with the tart cranberry juice, and swallowed. "Oh, no. Change the channel."

"Why?" He appeared genuinely confused.

"I don't really like watching myself on film. It just feels a little weird and egomaniacal to me."

He sat his empty plate aside. "Come on, now. There's nothing strange about enjoying the work you did." He scooted closer to her on the bed. "You're a talented actress, Sierra. Embrace that."

She sighed. "If you really want to watch it, I guess it's okay."

"Yes, I really want to watch it."

She finished her meal, half watching the drama unfolding on the screen. It was an episode that had originally aired about two weeks ago. They'd filmed eight more episodes since this one, and would soon wrap up filming for the season. During that episode, as with most of them, she'd had a lot of on-screen time with Mia.

Seeing Mia's face on the television made Sierra

cringe inwardly. She hadn't spoken at length to anyone but Jazmin about her issues with Mia. Though at this point, she was pretty sure everybody in the cast and crew could feel the tension between the two of them. For all Sierra knew, Mia could be telling anyone at the studio who would listen that she hated Sierra's guts. Mia was just petty enough to do that type of thing.

The show went to commercial break, and she blew out a breath.

He glanced at her, his brow furrowed. "What's the matter?"

She shook her head. "It's complicated. Suffice it to say there's a lot of drama at the studio, and the worst of it is playing out off-screen."

"Whatever it is, you can't be involved in it. I know you're too classy for that kind of thing."

Yeah, but Mia isn't. "You'd be surprised, Campbell."

He cleared the tray and dishes off the bed, and tugged her hand. "Come on. Get comfortable and tell me what's bothering you." He helped her change position in bed, until her back came to rest against the pile of pillows near the headboard.

Without going into too much detail, she told him about the ongoing tension between her and Mia. "I don't have any personal problem with Mia. She's been this way with me from the day we started working together, even though I've treated her with nothing but respect."

His frown told her he shared her frustration. "I can understand why you're stressed out about this. You're taking the high road with someone who obviously lacks maturity, and I know that must be difficult."

"Sometimes I wonder how much longer I can keep this up." She shook her head, feeling the tension gathering in her neck and shoulders. "I've been advised to just stay professional and wait until this blows over, but Mia is really testing the limits of my patience."

"I'm sorry I can't fix it for you."

His concern made her smile. "You're helping just by listening to me."

"Let me see what else I can do to improve your mood." The dark pools of his eyes displayed his desire.

She felt the tingle of anticipation dance down her spine. "What did you have in mind?"

"It's easier to show you." He moved then, kneeling on the bed beside her. He lifted her legs at the bend in her knees, easing them apart. He then raised the hem of her tee. His brow hitched. "Sierra, you naughty girl. You're not wearing any panties."

She trembled while his fingertips traced a lazy pattern on her inner thighs. "I didn't think I would need them."

"You were so, so right." He lay between her parted thighs, slipping his hands beneath her hips and raising her up to his mouth.

Her head fell back against the headboard as the first lick split her world in two. He followed it with more slow licks, soft suckles and lingering kisses until she thought she might die from the sheer pleasure of it.

When she shattered into bliss, he left her briefly to shed his shorts, then returned to lie atop her. She reached for him, pulling him into her arms as her legs wrapped around his waist and pulled him toward her core. She burned for him, and when he finally slid inside, her sigh was one of both relief and pleasure. They moved together, ruled by the storm of passion, until he roared his completion into the silence of the sunlit room.

Lying with him afterward, listening to his snores, she held his body close to hers. Running her fingers gently over the rippling curls of his close-cropped hair, she realized they were connected now, in all the ways a man and a woman could be. She'd shared her body, told her story and bared her soul to him. And now, she knew, he'd become a part of her.

Everything she'd believed about men, he challenged. Everything she thought she knew about relationships, he contradicted. But what would it mean to allow herself to care about him, to love him? It meant opening her heart to a pain she wasn't sure she could bear.

For now, she would settle for this moment and let that be enough. The present was all she had, because the past was gone and the future was yet to be. She didn't know what lay ahead of them, but she did know how she felt right now.

And right now, all she wanted was to spend the entire day in bed with him, before reality and responsibility separated them again.

Campbell sat in a booth at the Salty Siren later Sunday evening, drinking from a frosty mug of cola. Devon sat to his left and Savion occupied the leather bench on the other side of the table. Between them lay a spread of wings, onion rings and fries. When Devon had invited him to watch the football game at the sports bar, Campbell had accepted readily. The day had been long, and the pile of work seemed unending.

Savion, who'd caught Campbell on the way out the door and decided to join them, was once again staring into the pages of his leather-bound planner. He held the book aloft, so that no one at the table could see the pages, and scrawled in it with a pencil.

Campbell shook his head. "Savion. What are you writing in that damn book?"

"Noneya business." He erased something, then looked thoughtful for a moment before starting to write again.

Devon asked, "If you aren't going to watch the game, why'd you ask to join us, man?"

Savion shrugged. "I like the food here, and I didn't feel like cooking today."

"That's my brother, the sports fanatic." Campbell didn't bother trying to hide the sarcasm in his tone.

Savion, in his typical fashion, ignored his younger brother's comment.

Munching on an onion ring, Devon shook his head. "Y'all are a trip. Hadley told me to expect this kind of stuff when I told her you were both coming."

Savion rolled his eyes. "Sis has you on a short leash, huh, Devon?"

He shook his head. "Nah. I just texted her to let her know where I'd be. I'm considerate like that, bruh."

"Right. Sounds to me like Hadley's running things."

Devon shrugged. "Maybe, but when's the last time you had a woman, Savion?"

Instead of responding, Savion frowned and shut his planner, dropping it on the bench next to him.

Campbell laughed and fist-bumped Devon. "Solid burn, man." His older brother was way too serious, and needed to be set straight every now and then.

"You both know I love Hadley. She's the light of my life. So, if you're gonna tease me about loving her, and not being ashamed of it, so be it. But be prepared to have your ass handed to you."

Savion cracked a wry smile. "On the strength of my sister's happiness, I'll let you live."

Devon chuckled, then turned to Campbell. "Meanwhile, man, what were you doing over the weekend? I tried calling you Saturday afternoon and couldn't get you."

Campbell couldn't stop the grin from spreading over his face. "I was with Sierra."

Devon's face registered his surprise. "Really? And how did that go?"

"It went very well, trust me." He wasn't about to go into details, because he wasn't that kind of guy. He knew his friend would catch his meaning, without a full recap. "She's great, man. Really special."

"You mean the Ice Queen?" Savion crunched on a French fry. "Even those rich actor types in Hollyweird couldn't get next to her. You're telling me you won her over?"

He wanted to throw a chicken bone at his brother's head, but he restrained himself. "Yes, I did. So that means both Devon and I have way more game than you, bro."

Savion laughed. "Oh, please. You may be in good with her now, but don't expect it to last. You know how women are."

Campbell wondered why his brother had to be such a buzzkill. "You know, you love to take the wind out of people's sails, don't you?"

He shrugged. "It's a gift, I guess. But seriously, watch out with her. You stay in the ice palace long enough, you're bound to get frostbite."

Devon scoffed. "Oh, come on, Savion. You know that whole ice queen thing is just a label. It was something easy for the media to fixate on and run with. You know they always go for the low-hanging fruit."

That made Campbell think of something he'd

been wanting to ask. "By the way, Devon, how did this whole thing with her being called Ice Queen get started in the first place?"

"That's a good question," Savion said. "I don't remember a specific event, or even how long it's been. Yet I've been hearing the same story about her for years." He took a draw from his mug of beer.

Devon wiped his mouth, discarding the crumpled napkin. "This is how it went down. Several years ago, we worked together on a little indie film called *Tango at Dawn*. It was my second film and Sierra's first. Anyway, after we wrapped shooting, a reporter from one of those gossip rags comes on set. Now we were all exhausted, after being on the set for ten hours straight. This guy latches on to Sierra and won't let up."

Campbell's jaw tightened. "What was he after? A story, or her phone number?" Either way, he didn't like the idea of anyone harassing Sierra.

Devon shrugged. "I saw all this go down from a distance, so I didn't hear what he asked her. I know he followed her around the set for a good twenty minutes, though."

I'd love to punch this dude right in his throat. He didn't care for this nameless reporter, or his aggressive tactics. He made a mental note to ask Sierra about this whole thing later.

"She finally got sick of him and had security escort him off the lot. Two days later, his paper runs his story on the front page with the title Hollywood's Newest Ice Queen."

Savion asked, "Did you ever read the story, you know, to find out what he said?"

Devon shook his head. "Nah. Not about to give my money to a publication that would hire a creep like that. Sierra may have read it, though. Months later, when the reviews for the film came out, her performance was praised as one of the best of the year. Even got her nominations at a few film festivals."

"Wow. All of this was started by one overzealous reporter." Campbell shook his head.

"And because of the internet, the story probably lingers to this day. Since this all went down so early in her career, I suspect it's influenced the types of roles she's been offered." Devon shook his head. "It's kind of sad. I asked her to come do my show because I knew she'd be brilliant in the role, and she is. But I know she's looking to break out of that box she's been put in, and when the moment comes around, I'll be a hundred percent supportive."

Savion appeared somewhat surprised. "It's amazing what that little bit of bad press led to for her. I bought right into it, along with the masses."

"That's how it is, man. Media holds a lot of power over us, and that's true no matter how it changes form." Devon put his empty plate on the pile in the center of the table. "Magazines, blogs, gossip reporters all say the same kind of thing about Sierra.

But I've known Sierra for years and that's not who she really is."

Rubbing his chin, Campbell thought about everything he'd just heard. *I definitely need to sit down with Sierra and talk with her about this.* He hadn't wanted to probe into the details of the way she'd been stereotyped, thinking it would be better to get to know her as a person rather than dwelling on her public image. Now that he could see how much it might be affecting her, he realized he needed to know more. And he needed to hear it straight from the source.

Devon tapped his shoulder. "Look, Sierra's been through a lot, and I consider her a friend. I hope your intentions with her are good."

Campbell blinked a few times at the irony of the moment. "Didn't I have this same conversation with you last year, about your intentions with Hadley?"

Devon laughed. "Yeah, man, you did. So now the tables have turned. Sierra's grown and can do as she pleases. But if you hurt her, it'll be my pleasure to kick your ass."

Campbell rolled his eyes, but laughed anyway. "Understood, Devon."

On the other side of the table, Savion remarked, "Y'all are letting these women get under your skin way too much."

Campbell eyed him. "Don't worry, big brother. Your time is coming around."

Chapter 11

Sierra lay stretched out on the sofa Monday afternoon, watching television. She'd been home since noon, having wrapped filming for the day early, and was using her time off to binge-watch episodes of *Living Single*, one of her all-time favorite shows. The show, which had its original run from 1993 to 1998, explored the friendships of six young black professionals who lived in the same Brooklyn brownstone. Though she'd spent most of her acting career performing dramatic roles, she loved a good comedy.

As she listened to the on-screen exchange where Overton called Regine "Lil' Chief Running Mouth" for what had to be the hundredth time, she burst out laughing. *This show never gets old.* With all the things going on in her life right now, she needed this time to just kick back, watch her favorite nineties sitcom and crack up.

Her phone, lying facedown on the coffee table, buzzed again, and she sighed. *That damn thing has been buzzing all day.* She'd checked the screen a few times, to be sure it wasn't anything important. All she'd seen were a bunch of social media notifications, so she ignored them. She'd been given a reprieve in the form of a rare early wrap to filming, so she planned to take full advantage of it by unplugging from the rest of the world.

Picking the phone up, she tapped the screen, with the intent of clearing her notification tray. Instead, she opened one of the social media apps. The screen filled with tagged posts, and as she scrolled through, she felt the knot of tension forming between her shoulder blades. Every post was maligning her in some way, calling her everything from old, to ugly, to a "trash actress." She checked her other three accounts at different social sites and found much the same thing. While she deleted the messages from her feeds and blocked or reported some of the accounts posting those awful things, she couldn't help noticing that Mia kept appearing. Some of the posts originated from Mia's profiles; others had simply tagged her.

She was still busy cleaning out her social media streams when the phone started buzzing in her hand. This time it wasn't a notification, but a call, and she saw her mother's face appear on the screen. Swiping to answer, she said, "Hey, Mommy."

"Hi, Sugar Plum. How are you?"

Sierra smiled at the sound of her mother's familiar greeting. "I'm doing okay, Mommy."

"Hmm. You don't sound like it. What's the matter?"

In typical mom fashion, Rachel Dandridge had noticed her daughter's sullen mood. "It's nothing, Mommy. It's just that I've been filming a lot lately and I'm really tired."

"I see. Well, I hope you're getting some rest."

"I am. We wrapped filming before lunch today and I've been on the couch ever since."

"Mmm-hmm. Good." She paused. "So now that I know you're resting, why don't you tell me what's really bothering you?"

She sighed. Seeing no point in being dishonest with her mother, she said, "There are some ugly things being said about me on social media right now, and it's got me feeling a little stressed out."

"Social media?"

"You know, those online sites where people go to talk to their high school classmates and share cat videos."

"Oh, yes. Daddy and I don't bother too much with the computer you bought us, so we don't do any of that. What are they saying that's got you so upset?"

"Just a bunch of petty insults. I feel pretty certain that my costar is the one encouraging this type of negative conversation about me."

Rachel harrumphed. "That little young thing with the attitude? The one that's been rude to you on set? Why, I've got a good mind to call the studio, and tell them—"

Sierra stopped her. "Mommy, don't. It's not that big of a deal. I'll handle it."

"Are you sure? Because I'm not about to have people out here talking trash about my Sugar Plum."

She smiled at her mother's strong protective instincts. "I appreciate that, Mommy. But I promise I'll take care of it, okay?"

"Alright, Sierra. If you say so."

Changing the subject, she asked, "Have you had a chance to see the show yet?"

"Oh, yes. I've been watching and it is something else! All the girls in my bridge club are talking about it. You've definitely got a hit on your hands."

Sierra chuckled at the thought of her mother's bridge club watching the show together. The women were all retirees from the claims department of the insurance company her mother had worked for, and had been present throughout most of Sierra's life. "I'm glad you all are enjoying it."

"We are. And so is everybody else, from what I've seen. I read an article about it in the *LA Times*, and they're calling the show a top contender for the Emmys next year. They also say you're a shoe-in for best supporting actress in a drama."

"You know I don't read the reviews, Mommy."

"I know you don't. That's why I'm telling you."

Rachel giggled. "I know it took me and your daddy a while to come around to the idea of you being an actress. But I have to say, we sure are proud of you, Sugar Plum."

"Thanks, Mommy."

"You're welcome." She laughed again. "You know, thinking back on how you were as a little girl, we really should have picked up on your talent for acting. Remember how you carried on about those cello lessons? How you threw yourself across the foot of our bed and tried to stage a mutiny?"

"Yes, I remember." She'd been dead set against taking lessons on the instrument. "But you and Daddy would not be moved, and you made me take the lessons anyway."

"And it paid off, didn't it?"

"Yes. I ended up playing a cellist in my fourth film." She changed position on the sofa, facing the glass doors that led to the terrace. "That was just luck, though, Mommy. Meanwhile, I've yet to be offered a role with any lines in Mandarin Chinese."

"Oh, no, honey. That was a strategic decision. You see, when you take me and Daddy on vacation to Beijing one day, you'll be able to get us everything we need."

She laughed. "Really, Mommy?"

"Yes, child. I never joke about international travel."

"And when would I be taking you two on this trip?"

"Our fortieth wedding anniversary is coming up." She covered the receiver, and Sierra heard a muffled conversation going on in the background. "Your daddy says he'd be fine with going then."

Shaking her head, Sierra said, "Okay. As long as my filming schedule allows it, I'll take you."

"That's my Sugar Plum." She cleared her throat. "While I have you on the phone, let me ask you something. Are you seeing anybody?"

Unsure of how to answer that, Sierra said, "Nothing serious, Mommy."

"Okay. I'm not going to dig into your business. But don't forget that me and your daddy would like a grandchild, before we get too old to enjoy one."

Sierra sighed. "I gotta go, Mommy. I love you."

"I love you, too. Isn't it funny how you always have to go when I mention grandchildren?" She laughed once more before disconnecting the call.

Sierra set the phone down and turned her attention back to her show. By the time she'd watched another two episodes, the frequency of the notifications started to die down. But she was still getting far more of them than she wanted. She wondered if her agent would have some tips or resources on how she could be more proactive on her social accounts. Maybe then she could put the kibosh on this kind of thing before it got out of hand.

All this negative talk is really making me nervous. While the threats themselves didn't pose any physical threat to her, she knew better than to keep ignoring them. Crazy people were lurking in all the dark corners of the internet, waiting to be goaded into doing something in the real world. She didn't want any of the online foolishness to spill over into her actual life.

Picking up the phone again, she opened the dial pad and punched in Campbell's number. It was time to revisit the issue of her personal security.

Campbell was standing by his stove, flipping a turkey burger in the skillet, when his phone went off in his pocket. Setting down his spatula, he pulled the phone out and answered. "Hello?"

"Campbell, hi. It's Sierra."

He smiled. "How are you?"

"I've been better. That's why I wanted to give you a call."

He could hear something in her tone of voice that worried him. "What's up? Do you need something?"

"Do you remember when I asked you if you could get me a security guard?"

He thought back. "Yes, I remember that. I put in a few calls to a couple of agencies on the mainland, but I never heard anything back."

"Did you follow up with any of them?"

He wasn't a fan of the accusatory way she'd asked the question, but gave her an honest answer, one he knew she wouldn't like. "No. It takes a little time to set up things like this, so I didn't expect to hear back right away."

"Campbell, I really need a security detail. If

you're not going to make it happen for me, then just tell me who I need to contact to get it done."

He ran a hand over his face. "Tell me what brought this on, Sierra."

"I've been getting a lot of negative comments online, including some threats. Now, I know most people on these websites are just full of bluster, but you never can tell who the crazy ones are." She sighed. "I need to get some protection in place, in case someone decides to act on their nutty impulses."

He could tell she was genuinely concerned, and he felt a little guilty for not doing more to fulfill her request for security. "Okay, I understand your concern. I don't want you to feel unsafe. So here's what I'll do. I'll put in a call to Jarrod Riordan, our chief of police, and ask him if he has any men he can spare for a security detail for you."

"How soon can you call him?"

He glanced at the black acrylic wall clock mounted above his pantry door. "It's after six, so he's probably gone home for the day. We're old high school baseball teammates, and we talk every so often. I have his cell number. I can call and iron this out right now, then call you back. How does that sound?"

She seemed relieved. "That sounds great. Thank you for doing this for me."

"No problem. I hope we can work something out to your satisfaction."

With a naughty edge to her voice, she asked,

"Are you speaking as the property manager, or as my lover?"

He smiled, leaning against his kitchen counter as he thought of all the ways he could take her mind off her troubles. "Both."

"Sounds promising. Call me back when you've got some information."

"I will." He disconnected the call. Turning back to his turkey burger, he lifted the slightly charred patty out of the skillet and placed it on the bun he'd toasted earlier. After dressing the burger with lettuce, pickles and ketchup, he added a handful of plain potato chips and a tall glass of iced tea and took his meal to the table in his breakfast nook. Seated on the bench, he ate, so he could talk to Jarrod without chewing in the man's ear or being forced to listen to his own growling stomach. After he emptied his plate, he propped his feet up on the padded seat of the bench and dialed Jarrod's number.

"Yo, Campbell. Haven't heard from you in a minute. What's up, man?"

"Hey, Jarrod. I'm good, brotha. Just swamped with work. How have you been?"

"Doing fine. You know we're still hiring on more officers to match up with the population boom. Other than that, it's business as usual at SSPD."

"Yeah, I hear you." He sipped from his glass of tea. "Listen, I got a small favor to ask you."

"What do you need?"

"Sierra Dandridge is staying in one of the units at The Glenn, and she wants a personal security guard."

Jarrod chuckled. "Fine as she is, I can guess why. She probably has to beat guys off with a stick twenty-four/seven."

Campbell ignored the twinge of jealousy that flashed over him. *We're not in a relationship, so let me chill.* "That's true, but that's not her issue right now. She's getting some threats online, plus she's catching all kinds of attitude from her costar. She's nervous, and I don't blame her, based on what she's described to me."

"Hmm." Jarrod seemed to be analyzing what he'd just heard. "I feel you. Have you reached out to any agencies in Wilmington, or somewhere else on the mainland?"

"I have, but nobody's hit me back yet. Meanwhile Sierra's getting pretty antsy. Do you think you can help me out?"

"I'm not sure, Campbell. With the population growing the way it has been lately, I'm already short-handed. I've got interviews back-to-back all week to try and get some more people on the force."

Campbell scratched his head. "What about one of your newer recruits? You know, somebody that doesn't have an official beat yet?"

He could hear the keystrokes as Jarrod typed on his computer. "I did just have a new officer come in. Fresh out of school, too. I can give him this assignment, but only on a part-time basis. Will that work?"

Campbell straightened up in his seat. "Yes, it will. It probably won't be permanent, and I'll cut him loose as soon as we can get somebody full-time."

"Alright. I'll email you the details on him, and Ms. Dandridge can work out the specifics with him."

"Thanks, man. I appreciate it."

"No problem."

Campbell chatted with Jarrod for a few more minutes, then hung up. Hoping this news would help alleviate some of Sierra's stress, he called her back to let her know what he'd found out. She seemed pleased with what he told her, and promised to get in contact with the young officer as soon as Campbell forwarded his information.

After he'd gotten off the phone with her, he went upstairs to his bedroom to change. His split-level home, located about five miles from his parents' house, sat on a small hill in the Cooper Villas neighborhood. He'd chosen an older home, rather than having one constructed, because he loved the charm of the place. It had been built in the seventies and remodeled in the early two thousands right before he purchased it. While Savion and Hadley had gone for newer, larger properties, he'd bucked the trend. The house had plenty of space for a single man, and enough bedrooms to make it a nice starter home if he ever had a family.

A family. He didn't know if he'd ever get to the place where he felt comfortable with the idea of being someone's father. Being a husband, on the other hand, seemed less frightening. That was especially true now that he and Sierra had...

Wait a minute. What are we, anyway?

There'd been no commitments, no terms laid out in advance, no declarations between them. They'd simply been two adults acting on their mutual desire. And here he was, thinking about marriage as he rifled through his drawers to find his running clothes.

He pushed the thoughts away when he found what he'd been looking for. Stripping off the button-down shirt and slacks he'd worn to work, he put on a long-sleeved white tee, gray sweatpants and running shoes. Connecting his earbuds to his phone and starting up his run playlist, he left the house.

While running through the neighborhood, he listened to the hip-hop bass line pounding in his ears, using it to regulate his speed. In his mind's eye, he saw Sierra lying across his bed, beckoning to him with a crooked finger. He smiled, marveling at her ability to rule his mind the way she did. He enjoyed his memories of the smell of her, the taste of her, the feel of her body wrapped around his like a cocoon of warm silk.

I love her, don't I. It seemed inevitable, unavoidable. Now he had to figure out what to do, and when and how to tell her.

Directing his thoughts elsewhere before his desire impeded his ability to walk, let alone run, he turned the corner and picked up speed.

Outrunning his thoughts of her turned out to be much harder than he'd anticipated.

Chapter 12

It was back to business Tuesday, and Sierra arrived at the studio around 10:00 a.m. for several hours of filming. When she got to the main soundstage, she met with Devon and Aaron Tarlton, the show's director.

"Good morning, guys." Sierra dropped her purse in the folding chair embroidered with her name. "What are we shooting today?"

"Promos, and your last scene for this season." Aaron, seated in his chair, looked up from the bound script in his hand. "It's you and Grayson for the scene, and just you for the promos."

"So, Mia's not on set?"

Devon shook his head. "No, and she's not due for filming at all today."

"Great." Sierra felt the tension leave her body. Knowing she wouldn't have to deal with Mia's attitude would help her start the day off on the right note.

Grayson Richardson walked over then. Tall and handsome, with a medium skin tone and piercing gray eyes, Grayson was considered a heartthrob. Sierra liked him in a friendly way, but he wasn't her type. Cast in the role of Xander Lasalle, Fiona's brother, the veteran actor had plenty of television roles under his belt. "Hey, Sierra. Ready for this scene?" He gave her a dramatic wink.

"I'm ready, Grayson." She knew his teasing referred to the climactic scene they'd be filming today. "I've got my lines down, and I know just what to do."

"Great. See you over there." Grayson took a swig from his water bottle and headed toward the living room set where the scene would be filmed.

Sierra turned back to Aaron. "The writers have really gone all the way with this plotline. How do you think the viewers are going to react to this Karen and Xander pairing?"

Aaron chuckled. "Some will love it, and others will hate it. We figure about a sixty-forty split. Either way, it will do just what we want—get the viewers talking about the show."

I wonder what Mia thinks. She assumed Mia had read the script by now, that is, if she bothered to read the pages of scenes she wasn't included in. Sierra had a feeling that Mia wouldn't care for her character's brother and nemesis becoming romantically linked.

"Sierra, they're ready for you in the makeup chair."

Hearing the voice calling her from backstage, she excused herself and went to the prep area to get styled for filming. Passing the craft services table, she grabbed a cake doughnut and a bottle of water. She ate the doughnut while the wardrobe stylist fussed over her clothes. While the hairstylist curled her hair, she sipped from the water bottle. The makeup artist worked her magic last, completing the final step of Sierra's transformation into the duplicitous Karen Drake.

Under the bright lights, Sierra performed her scene with Grayson, delivering her lines with the flair and precision she was known for. As the scene came to an end, she leaned into Grayson's embrace as the script had dictated, and let him kiss her on the lips.

The moment their lips touched, she burst out laughing.

"Cut!" Aaron shouted.

Grayson gave her the side-eye. "What are you doing, Sierra?"

"Sorry. Let's run that again." She tamped down her mirth, drawing a deep breath. She was having a difficult time separating the sweet, goofy Grayson from his on-screen persona. Aside from that, kissing him felt strange, when she would rather be kissing Campbell.

Aaron's voice came through the megaphone.

"Take it from the last line through the kiss, please. Action!"

Sierra rolled through the line with no problem, but as Grayson leaned in to kiss her, she giggled.

"Cut!" Aaron appeared both surprised and annoyed. "Sierra, are you alright?"

She drew another slow, deep breath. "Sorry. A bit distracted."

"Are you ready, or should we take five?" Aaron's face displayed his distaste for the second option.

"I'm ready. Let's do it." Sierra looked at Grayson, who gave her a crooked grin.

"Last line through the kiss. Action!"

Sierra climbed out of her own skin and into Karen's, and when the kiss came this time, she melted into it as her character's emotions demanded. This was the part of acting she loved most, when she could truly connect with her role and leave her own issues and thoughts behind. They finished the scene without a hitch.

"Cut!"

Sierra and Grayson were both so deep in character that only Aaron's shouted command broke up the kiss.

"Perfect! That's a wrap!" Aaron smiled, and started clapping. His action started a round of applause, with the entire crew cheering.

"You're not half-bad, Sierra." A grinning Grayson bumped fists with her.

"You'll do, if nobody else is available." She elbowed him playfully.

He feigned injury. "Looks like my work here is done. See you later, Sierra."

She waved as he disappeared into the backstage area. Walking over to the director's chair, she said, "What's next?"

"Take a half-hour break, then be back here to shoot promos." Aaron turned the page on his script.

"Sure thing." She grabbed her purse and left the set, headed down the corridor toward her dressing room.

Jazmin met her, coming from the postproduction wing in the opposite direction. "Hey, girl. What's up?"

"I'm on a short break, then I'm doing promos. What are you doing?"

"Taking a break from editing episode footage. I've been in the booth since eight this morning, and I needed to stretch my legs."

She leaned against the wall, wanting to leave the path free for anyone who might pass by.

Jazmin leaned next to her. "So, have you had any more trouble out of Mia?"

"Not in person. She's not in the studio today."

Jazmin's brow furrowed. "What do you mean by 'not in person'?"

She gave her a brief recap of some of the things she'd seen on her social media feeds the day before. "I really don't go on there much—my assistant posts for me most of the time. She knows not to respond to negative posts, though. My phone was going off all day, and eventually I couldn't ignore it."

Jazmin shook her head. "This is getting way out of hand. I get that Mia's jealous, but why does she feel the need to get so out of pocket?"

Sierra shrugged. "I have no idea. I'm getting a security detail set up for myself, just in case, though."

"This sounds like a lot of stress." Jazmin leaned closer. "Look, if you want me to report her to the production staff, I will. I don't like seeing you go through all this trouble over her foolishness."

"You said yourself that if we report her, she'd probably get kicked off the show."

"Yes, but she can't keep doing the things she's doing, Sierra."

"I know." She sighed. "But I also know what it's like to get bad press when your career is just getting started. It will follow you for the rest of your days."

Jazmin touched her shoulder. "Are you sure about this, Sierra?"

She nodded. "Yes. Just let me talk it over with her, give her a chance to pump her brakes before she derails her career. You can mediate for us. Deal?"

"Sure. Just let me know the time and place." Jazmin started walking again. "I'm going to take a lap or two around the courtyard, and shake off this stiffness."

"Later." She continued walking toward her dressing room, Jazmin's words echoing in her mind: *She can't keep doing the things she's doing, Sierra.*

She knew Jazmin was right. But something inside her wanted to give Mia a chance to redeem herself, no matter how rude and unprofessional she'd been in the past.

Alone in her dressing room, she heard her phone buzz. Taking a bite of a granola bar, she took the phone out of her purse, half expecting to see another crass comment from one of her social media accounts.

Instead, she saw a text message from Campbell.

Miss you. Hope you're having a good day.

She typed a reply.

It just got a lot better.

He sent back another message. Dinner tonight?

She smiled. Pick me up at the studio at six. Should be done by then.

Sounds great. See you later.

Tucking the phone away, she sat back on her love seat. Things at work were still a bit crazy, but things with Campbell were going great.

I can't wait to see him tonight.

Campbell came to the studio at six, just as Sierra had asked. He sat in the parking lot for a few minutes, waiting for her to come out. When he saw her, he got out and held open the passenger side door for her. She looked beautiful in her white slacks and blazer, paired with the bright blue shell and matching pumps. Her hair was down, falling over her left eye in a very enticing style that framed her face well.

"Sorry, I'm a few minutes late. Those promos were a killer." She settled into the seat.

"No problem." He shut the door behind her.

Soon they were on the road. The evening, beautiful and warm, presented perfect cruising weather, so he'd left the top down on his convertible. Out of the corner of his eye, he caught a glimpse of her silvery lavender hair whirling around her head in the wind. Her expression conveyed calm, and knowing all the stress she dealt with, he enjoyed seeing her relaxed.

"Do you like seafood, Sierra?"

She nodded. "I love it. Especially salmon."

"Great. You're going to love this place." He was glad she hadn't said she didn't like seafood, as that was tantamount to blasphemy on the island.

They pulled into the lot at Shoreside Grill, and he escorted her inside. The hostess led them to a reserved table, one that provided a great view of the rolling waves of the Atlantic through the large window.

After the waiter had taken their orders and collected their menus, Campbell asked, "How was your day at the studio?"

She recapped her time on set. "It was a pretty good day, overall. I just wish I hadn't been so unfocused with Grayson at the end of our scene."

"What happened?"

She looked away for a moment. "I had to...kiss him."

His raised an eyebrow. "I'm confused. Why was that a problem?"

"It wasn't. It's just that I know Grayson, and he's a total goofball. He's rarely ever serious. It was hard to imagine him as a master of seduction." She sipped from her glass of water. "Luckily, I got it together after a couple of takes."

Campbell shook his head. "I'm shocked. The great Sierra Dandridge, unfocused?"

She chuckled. "I know. It seems unbelievable. I've kissed other actors for scenes before, and I thought I'd gotten used to it. Today was different, though."

His phone buzzed, and he turned it to silent and put it in the pocket of his slacks. "How so?"

She reached across the table to grasp his hand. "I just kept thinking about how I'd rather be kissing you."

His heart thudded in his ears. "You flatter me, fair lady."

"It's true." She gave his hand a squeeze, then released it. "I don't know what to call this thing that's happening between us, but it's impossible to ignore."

He shrugged. "I understand that. But who says we have to define this? Why can't we just enjoy each other's company, and leave it at that?"

She nodded, smiled. "I like the way you think, Campbell."

He raised his water glass in salute.

The waiter returned with their steaming plates, setting them down on the table before disappearing. She looked at her cedar plank salmon entrée and rubbed her hands together. "This looks fantastic."

"You'll love it. Best salmon in town, bar none." He spread his white linen napkin over his lap, then picked up his fork to get a taste of his own lemon pepper trout.

"Tell me about your day." She chewed a bite of food as she waited for his response.

"Let's see. It was pretty typical. Did a stack of paperwork about four feet high. Met with two clients about rental units. Sat through the longest, most boring staff meeting ever."

She laughed. "Sounds pretty rough."

"Not rough. Just…dull as all hell." He washed down a few bites with a swig of water. "I do have some news for you, about your condo."

"What?"

"I've had the security company there all morning, upgrading your unit's system. You now have cameras aimed at the front door, and the glass door that goes out to the terrace."

"That's great. Thank you for doing that. But I thought there wasn't any outside access to the terrace?"

"There isn't. We put the camera up anyway, in case some nut decides to scale the trellis or something." He winked, hoping she'd realize he was joking.

She giggled. "I appreciate the forethought."

"No problem. When I take you home, I'll show you how to operate the keypad. The cameras are monitored at the guard booth, at the security company's headquarters in Wilmington and through a closed-circuit channel you can access from any television inside the unit."

"Wow. Sounds pretty state-of-the-art."

"Did you get in touch with Roland?"

She nodded. "I did. I spoke with him this morning before I went to the studio. Thanks for connecting me with him."

"You're welcome, though a good deal of the credit goes to Jarrod. Have you two worked out a schedule yet?"

"We've started to. He's going to start Thursday, and we'll iron it out further then."

They ate the rest of their meal in companionable silence. By the time the waiter collected their empty plates, Campbell was ready for something sweet. "Want to order dessert?"

She patted her stomach. "I don't know. I'm *so* full."

"We could share something."

She thought about it. "Okay, but nothing too rich or heavy."

"I know just the thing." He flagged down the waiter.

When the large, nut-filled brownie topped with a dollop of whipped cream arrived, she looked at him. "Are you serious?"

He shrugged. "It's the lightest dessert they have." He moved to sit on her side of the booth, scooting close to her on the seat. Grabbing one of the forks, he cut off a piece of the brownie and held it to her lips. "Open up, honey."

She laughed, but did as he asked. After the first bite, she made a moaning sound low in her throat. "Oh, my goodness, that's delicious."

"I'm glad you like it." He realized he could get used to hearing her make that sound, especially if he was the one to inspire it.

"Your turn." She forked up a piece of the brownie and fed it to him.

The soft, chewy texture seemed to melt in his mouth, giving way to the deep chocolate flavor and the crunch of the walnuts inside. "Mmm."

They carried on that way, each feeding the other a bite or two, until only crumbs remained on the white ceramic plate.

She fell back against the seat. "Okay, now I know I can't eat another bite. I may have to fast till next week so I can get into my jeans."

"To be fair, they were already fitting you pretty snugly." He chuckled. "But that's the way I like them."

She gave him a soft punch in the shoulder. "Watch yourself, playboy."

He paid the bill, and escorted her back to his car.

On the way to her condo, she didn't say much, seeming content to keep her own counsel and enjoy the passing scenery. He loved the way she looked in the shadow of dusk, and stole glances at her at every opportunity. *She's amazing.* He could feel himself slipping into a realm he'd never been in before. He'd loved Tiffany, yes. But the things he had started to feel for Sierra went far beyond that. So far, in fact, that it made him a little nervous.

Back at the condo, he walked her upstairs and demonstrated how to work the keypad to the upgraded security system, just as he'd promised. "Do you feel comfortable using it?"

She nodded. "I think so. It's a lot to remember, though."

He pointed to the laminated sheet on the coffee table. "The installer left you a quick reference card, in case you get confused. The website for the company is on there, as well, so you can check there if you need to." He closed the plastic cover over the keypad. "And you know you can always call me, if you need help right away."

"Got it. Thanks, Campbell." She leaned up and placed a soft kiss on his cheek.

He kissed her back, on the lips. "If I didn't have a ton of work waiting for me tomorrow, I'd ask if I could stay the night."

Her long eyelashes fluttered enticingly. "And if you didn't have so much work, I'd let you."

"You have no idea how tempting you are. But I've got an early meeting at 8:00 a.m. sharp."

They shared another lingering kiss, and he enjoyed holding her close to him for as long as he could.

Then he left, stepping out into the cool night air and closing the door behind him.

As he jogged down the steps, he knew he'd made the right decision, even though it had been difficult to leave her.

Because if he stayed, he might say the three words that had been on the tip of his tongue. And he wasn't sure either of them were ready for that.

Chapter 13

Though she'd finished her filming for the season, Sierra went to the studio on Wednesday anyway. She'd asked Jazmin to arrange a meeting with Mia, so they could hash out the issues between them once and for all. She wasn't looking forward to the meeting, but she knew it was better to get it out of the way now rather than put it off and risk having things escalate.

Inside the studio, she went to the office adjoining the postproduction booth, a neutral area chosen by Jazmin. She'd thought it would be better to do it there than in a more public area, in case things went downhill.

Sitting in one of the upholstered chairs at the conference table, Sierra drummed her fingers on the desk. Looking to Jazmin, who sat at the head of the table, she asked, "You did tell her what time to be here, right?"

Jazmin nodded. "Yes. She's already on set, so I'm sure she'll be here any minute."

Sierra sighed and continued her drumming. *I just wish she'd hurry up, so we can get this over with.*

About ten minutes later, Mia sashayed into the room in her usual dramatic fashion. In contrast to Jazmin's and Sierra's casual jeans-and-top attire, Mia wore a strapless, mint-green maxi dress festooned with crystals around the neckline and hem. Sitting across from Sierra at the table, Mia lifted the huge, jewel-encrusted sunglasses from her eyes and set them atop her close-cropped hair.

"Hey, Jazmin." Mia's cold glare shifted her way. "Sierra."

"Hello, Mia." Sierra met her gaze without flinching.

Jazmin spoke. "Okay, ladies, let's handle this. We like to keep a positive, professional environment at our studios. So, let's hash this out. Who wants to go first?"

Sierra nodded toward Mia. "She can go first, if she wants." Mia struck her as a girl who truly enjoyed the sound of her own voice.

"Age before beauty," Mia droned, making a sweeping gesture toward Sierra.

Here we go with this crap. She pursed her lips. "Fine, I'll go. I don't have any problem with you,

Mia. I just don't like the way you act toward me. I've never done anything to you, and yet you seemed to have a problem with me from our first interaction."

Mia shrugged. "I'm not saying you've done or said anything to me. I just don't like you."

"But why?" Jazmin asked. "This really doesn't make any sense."

"Our chemistry is off, or whatever." Mia folded her arms over her chest. "Everybody isn't going to like you. Haven't you ever heard that before?"

Sierra leaned forward. "Trust me, Mia. I truly don't care whether you like me or not. I don't need or want your approval. What I'm asking for is basic respect and professionalism."

Mia leaned in, as well, matching her stance. "Listen here, old lady. I know you think you're hot shit because you've got a few movies under your belt. I don't owe you anything." She narrowed her eyes, punctuating her next words by stabbing her long fake fingernails against the surface of the table. "I don't like you, Sierra. And it's not gonna change."

Sierra felt the heat of anger rising in her blood. "The only one here who thinks they're hot shit is you. You've got a lot to learn if you want to have any longevity in this industry, Mia. It all starts with attitude, and yours is absolute garbage."

Mia stuck her finger in the air, dangerously close to Sierra's face. "Heifer, I—"

Jazmin slapped her hand on the table and stood. "Mia, that's enough."

Mia turned wide, surprised eyes on the producer.

"You heard me. I'm sick of this crap. You've been nothing but a brat to Sierra since you two started filming together. You're an embarrassment to the cast and crew of this show. We've all seen it, and everyone agrees that you are the source of the problem."

Mia's face turned beet red. "What are you saying, Jazmin?"

"I'm saying I'm going to make a recommendation to Devon to release you from your contract, Mia."

She hopped to her feet, shivering with what looked like outrage. "You can't do that! I'm the star!"

"The reviews say otherwise." Jazmin propped her hands on her hips. "Besides, we've wrapped all your scenes for the season. We've got plenty of time to replace you before we start filming again."

"Fine," Mia snapped, already headed for the door. Before she left, she set a venomous glare on Sierra. "You'll pay for this." Then she stomped into the corridor.

Jazmin strode to the door, calling out behind her, "Clean out your dressing room, Ms. Leigh."

Sierra released a long, deep sigh. "Damn it. I didn't want it to go like this, Jazzy."

Reentering the office, Jazmin patted her shoulder. "I know you didn't. It's not your fault. You were more than patient with her. Apparently, Ms. Leigh just doesn't want to work on this show. And if she doesn't improve her attitude, she won't be working anywhere else, either."

Shaking her head, Sierra leaned back against her chair. When the press got wind of Mia's firing, and the details surrounding it, they'd drag her name through the proverbial mud.

Jazmin was right. She'd tried to work things out with Mia, but the girl just wouldn't be moved. So here they were. "I just hope her replacement has a better attitude."

"There's a good shot she will," Jazmin remarked, pushing her chair up to the table. "Mia set the bar pretty damn low."

Later, back at her condo, Sierra lay across her bed, talking to Campbell on the phone. She relayed in detail what had happened at the studio. "It was crazy. I can't believe how Mia acted, right there in front of one of our producers. It was almost like self-sabotage."

"I don't know what's up with Mia, but it's pretty obvious she's got issues." He crunched on something, the sound reverberating in her ear. "At least she's out of your hair now."

She frowned as the noise intensified. "Geez, Campbell, what are you eating?"

"Roasted almonds." He stopped chewing. "Sorry. I'll put them away until after we finish talking."

"Thanks." She rolled over onto her left side. "Roland starts tomorrow at seven. He'll be guarding the door from then until midnight."

"Okay. I know he works days with the police department, so it's nice of you not to keep him all night."

"Yeah. Man's gotta sleep, right?" She yawned. "Excuse me. He's also going to be on call for me, and he'll be running through the social media pages of the people who've posted nasty things on my profile pages."

"Sounds good." He sounded distant, uninterested.

"Campbell, are you busy with something?"

"Nah. Just flipping through the sports page."

She frowned. She'd had a hell of a day, but if he wasn't into listening right now, she didn't want to burden him with her troubles. "I'll let you go. I'll text you tomorrow."

"Sounds good."

She shook her head at the repeated phrase. "Good night, Campbell."

"'Night, Sierra."

She disconnected the call and tossed her phone aside. Standing up, she went to the master bathroom to run a hot bath. Once she settled beneath the bubbles, her hair wrapped in a towel, she sighed with contentment. Campbell might not be interested in helping her relax, but she had other ways of relieving stress.

An hour later, she emerged from the tub, clean and refreshed. She slipped into a comfy, worn T-shirt and a pair of cutoff sweatpants. Padding barefoot down the hallway, she went to the kitchen and tossed herself a salad for dinner.

As she walked to the sink to rinse off her plate, she heard someone knocking at the door.

Her frazzled nerves rose to the surface again. She hadn't been expecting anybody. *Who's out there, and what the heck do they want?* She needed her peace and quiet right now, and was in no mood to entertain visitors.

She grabbed the stainless steel meat mallet from the kitchen, strode to the door and leaned in to look through the peephole.

Campbell draped the canvas grocery bag over the crook of his elbow and knocked on Sierra's door again. *I know she's here. Her car's parked right downstairs.*

The door swung open, and there she stood, wielding a meat mallet, eyes flashing.

"Whoa!" Campbell jumped back from the door. "Damn, Sierra, did I catch you at a bad time?"

She blinked a few times, staring at him for a moment. Then she seemed to relax, and lowered her weapon. "Sorry, Campbell. Why didn't you tell me you were coming over?"

"It was kind of a last-minute decision." He kept a little distance between them, letting his gaze sweep over her. She wore an old tee and a pair of cotton shorts, her hair wrapped up in a towel. Even in her comfy clothes and wielding a blunt object, she was still as lovely as a summer's day. "Can I come in?"

She blew out a breath, stepped aside. "Sorry about that. Come on in."

Once he was shut inside, he set his bag on the table. "You know, I'd really feel better if you put the meat mallet away."

She laughed, shook it in his direction. "You were ignoring me on the phone. I should give you a whack to teach you a lesson."

He held his hands out in front of him. "You're right, I wasn't listening. That's why I'm here, to offer an apology in person."

"I might accept it." She winked as she strolled to the kitchen to holster her weapon.

"I'd appreciate it. And I promise, if I ever do that again, feel free to tenderize me. I'll just stand and take my whacks like a man."

Her throaty laugh carried across the condo, reaching him before she did. "Campbell, you're crazy." She gestured to his bag on the table. "So, what did you bring?"

He reached into the bag and extracted the contents. "Massage oil and chocolate. I thought you might need a massage. And now that I'm here, and I've seen the look on your face when you opened the door, I *know* you need one."

"You're right. Come on in the bedroom. We can do it there."

He grinned. "I was hoping the massage would lead to that."

She walked past him, shaking her head. "Just come on, Campbell."

In the master suite, she stripped off her top and lay across the bed, naked from the waist up. He knelt next to her on the bed, squeezing some of the citrus-scented oil into the palm of his hand. He'd chosen this oil because it reminded him of her, and as he rubbed his hands together to warm the oil, the scent permeated the air around them.

"Mmm," she murmured against the comforter. "That stuff smells good."

"Glad you like it. I'll leave the bottle here when I'm done." Laying his palms over her back, he started kneading the muscles, feeling for knots of tension. He found a few near her shoulder blades, so he focused on that area for a while, hoping to knock out some of the kinks and help her relax.

"That feels wonderful."

"I know you had a rough day. We both did." Before he could tell her about what happened at the office, she started up again.

"I just can't believe Mia acted that way. She's really very immature for a woman her age."

"Some people just don't know when to exercise good sense."

"It's incredible. I mean, she's not bad as an actress. But her attitude is just a hot mess. She's got to get it together."

"You're right. The woman obviously needs a therapist or something. By the way, I—"

"I tried not to get her in trouble, tried to keep her from losing her job. She just wouldn't quit."

Neither will you. He kept massaging her, working down along her spine now. "I hear you, Sierra. But dwelling on it isn't going to help you or her. Now, if you really want to hear a story, let me tell you what happened at my office today—"

To his amazement, she interrupted him again, rambling on about what Mia had said to her. He shook his head. He could recall Tiffany's penchant for endlessly rehashing an event, and for interrupting him when he tried to speak. His ex-wife was the last thing he wanted to be thinking about while he was touching Sierra, but there it was. When it became clear she wasn't going to let him speak, he gave up trying and continued the massage in silence.

He pressed his fingertips against her tailbone, and she moaned low in her throat. "Oh, yes."

"Like this?" He applied deep, but gentle pressure to the spot.

She trembled beneath his touch. "Yes. That feels fantastic."

He loved giving her pleasure, loved hearing her say she liked what he did to her. He kept up his attention to that spot, until he felt the kink in the muscle wall melt away beneath his touch. "There. You should be feeling much better now."

"I am." She purred the words as she rolled over onto her back.

The sight of her breasts, with her nipples hard and wanting, made him suck in a breath. "Whew."

"Do you have any other tricks up your sleeve to relieve my tension, Campbell?" She stared at him with hooded, desire-filled eyes.

"I'll see what I can do." He leaned over to kiss her.

She wrapped her arms around his shoulders and drew him down into her embrace. "Then I leave myself in your very capable hands."

He nuzzled his lips against the warm hollow of her neck. "Something's happening between us, Sierra. Can you feel it, too?"

She didn't respond verbally, but she squeezed him tighter, closer to her heart.

He smiled. Holding her close for a few moments more, he finally admitted his truth aloud. "I love you, Sierra."

She looked up at him, her eyes damp and emotional, and gave him a quiet nod.

That was good enough for him. Choosing not to dwell on it, he let desire take over and answered the call of her body.

Chapter 14

Thursday night, Sierra met Campbell at Shoreside Grill again, this time for a double date with Hadley and Devon. They sat in the same booth as before, with each couple occupying one side of the table. Sierra did her best to keep her attention on the conversation, but she couldn't help thinking about what Campbell had said. *He loves me.* The weight of that had caught her so off guard she'd been unable to respond. Now she wondered what she would say when the subject inevitably came up again.

They'd been chatting easily throughout their meal. Over dessert, their conversation turned to the set of *The Shores*.

Devon, sipping coffee with his slice of cheesecake, remarked, "We let Mia go. We're already searching for her replacement."

Sierra shook her head. "I'm sorry it had to come to that, but like I told Campbell, she seemed determined to sabotage her own career."

"It's a sad situation, but she brought it on herself, based on everything Dev's been telling me." Hadley cut into her strawberry shortcake with a fork.

"So, what happens after you find a new actress to replace her?" Campbell asked. "Will you keep the same name for her character?"

Devon shrugged. "I'm not sure yet. We'll probably pull together a focus group from the viewers on social media and get their opinions. I've seen shows do that before. Remember Darren number one and Darren number two on *Bewitched*?"

Everyone at the table nodded.

"The reactions to things like that can be pretty mixed. I'm thinking of creating a new character, a half sister of Fiona and Xander. That way Grayson's character isn't affected by Mia's leaving the show. He shouldn't have to pay for her bad behavior."

Sierra nodded. "I agree. Grayson is a great guy, a professional through and through." She sipped iced water from her glass. "I like the idea of giving him a new half sister. How likely is that to happen, though?"

"Not sure yet. The other producers have to agree, and then we'll have to see what the writers can come up with. If everything works out like I hope, we can move forward with season two without too much inconvenience to the existing cast and crew."

"Hopefully it will be a smooth transition for the new actress, as well."

"Right." Devon polished off the last of his cheesecake. "The last thing we need is more drama on set. That could run her off before she ever films a scene."

Sierra gazed out the window. It was a windy evening, and the waves were crashing against the shore. "I hope Mia will get herself together. I really did try to keep things professional."

"We all know you did, Sierra." Hadley touched her hand. "Remember, hon. You can't save someone who doesn't want to be saved."

She nodded, acknowledging the truth in Hadley's words. She liked Campbell's baby sister. The two of them had spent time chatting on set, and had had lunch and coffee together when Sierra had time off but Devon was busy with things at the studio. Hadley was caring, considerate and honest, and it was easy to see why Devon loved her so much. If Mia had been more amenable, Sierra imagined they could have gotten to know each other on a friendly basis, as well.

Sierra wished she could put aside the twinge of guilt she felt about what had happened to Mia, but it remained, lurking in the corners of her mind. *I guess it will go away in time.*

"I expect the atmosphere will be much better on set now." Devon pushed his plate away and excused himself from the table. "Be right back."

Hadley leaned closer to Sierra. "Have you been onto your social media profiles lately?"

Sierra sighed. "No, but I can guess what they look like."

"Girl. Mia is out there acting a fool online, cursing your name to anyone and everyone." Hadley gestured to her phone. "It's a mess."

"I figured as much. That's why I haven't been checking."

Campbell reached for Hadley's phone. "Mind if I take a look?"

"Go ahead." She passed it to him.

Sierra watched Campbell's facial expression as he scrolled through the things displayed on the phone's screen. What started as confusion morphed into surprise, then anger. He passed the phone back to Hadley. "Sierra, you need to turn these posts over to Roland, so he can add them to the database at the police station."

Her eyes widened. "Are they really that bad?"

His face remained grim. "Let's just say Mia might have finally gone off the deep end."

Sierra nodded to indicate her understanding. *How in the world did I get into such a mess?* When she'd taken the job on the show, she'd been hoping to enjoy a new challenge. She'd done miniseries and made-for-television films, but never an ongoing series. And as much as she loved playing Karen Drake, the role had come with much more drama in her real life than she ever had on-screen.

Devon returned to the table then, and seemed to sense the mood. Sitting down, he asked his wife, "Baby, what happened? Y'all see a ghost while I was gone?"

Hadley shook her head. "I showed Campbell what's going on with Sierra's social media."

He answered with a solemn nod. "I see."

Sierra searched Devon's face. "You've seen the posts, too?"

"Yes. And I really think you should tell the police about what's going on."

"That's the same thing I just said," Campbell interjected.

"Take their advice, Sierra." Hadley drew a deep breath. "I'm worried."

Sierra took out her phone. "Don't worry, Hadley, I'm calling Roland right now." When he picked up, she let him know to collect her social media information from her assistant, and sweep the accounts for malicious activity. When she hung up, she reported what he'd said. "He's at my place now, but he's putting in the necessary calls, and he says he'll be on the lookout for anything suspicious."

"Good." Campbell sounded relieved. "Now that the police know about it, maybe they can put a stop to it."

"I hope so." Devon draped his arm over Hadley's shoulder. "Online bullying can be hard to prosecute. But if you need anything, anything at all, don't hesitate to ask us."

"Thank you, Devon. I really appreciate that."

Later, as she and Campbell sat on the sofa inside the condo, she said, "How did I get mixed up in all this, Campbell?"

He sighed. "I don't know, baby. Just a run of bad luck, I suppose." He gave her a squeeze. "Don't worry about it. I'm here for you."

"Didn't you tell me you were taking a few vacation days?"

He nodded. "Yeah. Finally got caught up on paperwork, so I don't have to go in tomorrow. Might take off Monday, too."

"I know it's short notice, but I'm headed up to New York tomorrow for a meeting. Would you like to come along?"

"It is short notice. But I don't mind. It's what, an hour's flight from Raleigh?"

"About. If you're willing to go, it won't cost you anything. The director I'm meeting is sending a private jet for me."

"Very fancy." He looked impressed.

"I agree. I usually fly commercial, but he offered, so I accepted."

"How long are you staying up there?"

She shrugged. "I'll probably fly back Saturday. I may take in a few sights, but I don't want to keep you away too long."

"Will I need business attire?"

"Nah. You don't have to come with me to the meeting, so you can wear whatever you like."

"Okay. If we leave for the airport early enough that I can grab some things from my house, I'm game." He yawned. "As for right now, I just want to lie here and hold you."

"No arguments here." She snuggled closer to him, pushing away her fears and letting his embrace be her balm.

Lying there in silence, she thought back on his declaration of love the night before. She'd heard him, and hadn't said anything back. He hadn't brought it up, so she didn't know what to think. *He's in love with me, and I don't know how I feel about him yet.*

Was it wrong for her to keep seeing him, while she was uncertain of her feelings? Was she leading him on, knowing he'd already invested his heart?

She cared about him, and she knew her feelings grew and deepened as she spent more time with him. Maybe she did love him. But saying it out loud would make it real... Perhaps a little too real.

She had lots of questions and no answers, so she tried to push the thoughts out of her mind. She needed him right now, in more ways than one.

She just hoped she didn't end up hurting him.

After their Friday morning flight to JFK, Campbell accompanied Sierra to the Plaza Hotel for her meeting with the director. Campbell kissed her on the cheek as she and her agent went into the meeting, then spent the next hour exploring the hotel and the surrounding block. He'd dressed comfortably in dark slacks and a solid blue button-down, and had no problem getting around in his leather walking loafers.

He met her back in the hotel lobby around two, as she'd requested. After they said goodbye to her agent, he asked, "How did the meeting go?"

"I think it went well, though the director was kind of hard to read." She shrugged. "If all goes well, he'll call me back with an offer."

"What's the movie about?" He held her hand as they stepped out into the afternoon sunshine.

"It's a romantic comedy. Just the kind of role I've been looking for to break out of the Ice Queen box."

He drew in a breath before asking his next question. "And the director? Was he…you know, professional with you?"

Her eyes said he knew what she meant, and she nodded. "Yes, he was a total gentleman. No creepy vibes at all."

He enjoyed the relief that flowed through him. "Well, I'm sure that if that director wants a box office hit, he will hire you, Sierra."

She smiled up at him. "Thanks, Campbell."

He winked. "So, what's on the agenda now?"

"How about we grab a late lunch? After that, there's a great jazz spot here in Manhattan that Jazmin told me about. I'd love to go there and hear some live music, if you're down,"

He wasn't a huge fan of jazz, but he found it hard to deny her anything. "Let's go."

She smiled, leading him toward the edge of the sidewalk to hail a taxi.

They ate a fabulous meal at a little family-owned restaurant, and took a walk around Central Park to burn off some of the calories. After that, they took a horse-drawn carriage ride to Smoke, a jazz spot she'd mentioned earlier. While they rode through the streets in the carriage, Campbell noticed people who stopped and pointed in their direction. Sierra smiled and waved at them as they snapped photos of her, looking like a queen greeting her public.

The club's interior impressed Campbell the moment they walked in. The long, redwood bar was worked by bartenders in black button-down shirts. Vintage crystal chandeliers hung overhead, and each one of the white-clothed tables was illuminated by candlelight. "Nice atmosphere."

"Yeah," Sierra remarked. "It's even nicer than Jazzy described."

The place was packed, and Campbell assumed it was like that most Friday nights. According to the board near the entrance, a jazz quartet would be performing in less than thirty minutes. "Looks like we got here just in time. A show's about to start."

She led him to the hostess stand. They lucked out, and were seated at one of the last available tables. "I just wish it wasn't so crowded in here," Sierra murmured.

"Me, too, but this is probably typical for a club on the Upper West Side on a Friday night."

She nodded, but still appeared uncomfortable. Her eyes darted around the room, as if she were searching for someone…or something.

"You alright?"

"Sure. I'm fine." She released a nervous little laugh. "I'm not a fan of crowds, and I like them even less since this whole mess with Mia."

He frowned. "You mean, you're an actress, and you don't like crowds?"

"It's one thing to be in front of a crowd for an event. It's an entirely different thing to be part of the crowd."

I never really thought about it that way, but I guess it makes sense.

"Besides, I don't do very many live appearances. I act in front of a camera, and no one is there but the rest of the cast and the crew. I record most of my interviews in advance. I very rarely do anything live, and when I do, it takes me a while to get my nerves together."

Wow. It seemed Sierra had a lot of layers still left to uncover. "Do you want to leave? I don't want you to be uncomfortable."

She shook her head. "We came all the way over here, and our flight back doesn't leave till morning. Let's at least stay for a few songs."

"Okay, if you're sure." He settled in for the show.

The quartet came out onstage and performed a laid-back set of jazz standards. Since he wasn't a fan of jazz, he was somewhat bored by what sounded like fancified live elevator music. Still, he tapped his foot in time with the music, all the while watching Sierra, to gauge her mood.

By the fifth song, her jitters seemed to get the better of her. She turned to him and placed her hand on his forearm. "I'm ready to go."

"Sure." Happy to take the reprieve from this dull music, he grabbed her hand and walked outside with her.

The hotel she'd booked for the night was within walking distance of the club, so they made their way up the block, weaving through the thick foot traffic. Along the way, a group of squealing, college-aged girls approached, and Sierra smiled as she signed autographs and posed for selfies with them.

Once they were safely in their room, Campbell leaned down to give her a kiss. "Need me to take the edge off, baby?"

She returned his kiss, but with a little peck, devoid of passion. "Thanks, Campbell. I just want to crawl into bed and get some sleep."

He nodded, and watched her disappear into the bathroom, shutting the door behind her. What was her deal? She seemed to be shutting down, and shutting him out. He'd forced himself not to contemplate when or if she'd admit she cared for him. Was this her way of letting him know she didn't return his feelings?

Lying across the bed, he stared at the ceiling and

wondered what to do next. If she really didn't love him, what would be the point of continuing to see her?

He shook his head. *I guess we'll have to iron all this out when we get back to the island.*

Chapter 15

Monday, Sierra sat on the terrace of the condo, staring out toward the inlet. Things had taken an awkward turn between her and Campbell Friday night. When she'd returned from the bathroom, he'd vacated the bed, choosing to sleep on the pullout sofa, so she could get some rest. The next morning's flight had passed mostly in silence, punctuated only by small talk. And she hadn't heard from him at all since they'd returned to the island.

She'd thought about calling him, to ask what the issue was, but decided against it. He'd professed his love for her, and she'd offered him very little in return. To her mind, that was what stood between them, and until she was ready to definitively say whether she felt the same, she had no right to make demands on him or his time.

She got a call from Devon, asking her to come down to the studio. When she arrived at Devon's office on the second floor, she walked across to his desk and sat down in one of the guest chairs.

"We think we've found a good fit to take Mia's place on the show, and I wanted to get your opinion."

She leaned forward. "Sure. Who do you have in mind?"

"We're thinking of asking Zola Revere. Are you familiar with her?"

She thought for a minute. "Wasn't she on that soap last year? What was it called?"

Devon filled in the blank. "The show is called *River's Edge*. And yes, that's her. We think she might be a good fit for the show, especially since she already has some experience working on a television drama."

"I've seen the show, and I have to agree. *River's Edge* is similar in tone to *The Shores*. Have you reached out to her agent?"

"Not yet, but we will over the next few days. We wanted to gauge the reactions of some of the cast members first. Grayson was in here earlier, and he's on board, as well."

She nodded. "Sounds good. Just let me know what happens, and if I can help out in any way." She stood, preparing to leave.

"There is one more thing."

"Sure, what is it?"

"Would you be willing to do some press today? I know you don't really like interviews, but it's all recorded. Nothing live."

She cringed. "Devon, how important is this?"

"Very. You've seen how Mia's acting online. We need to get ahead of the story before the media spins it into something that reflects negatively on you, and the rest of the cast."

She sat back down in the chair, thinking. "I can see how this could go bad. Mia might try to create a narrative that makes her look like the injured party, railroaded by her mean and jealous coworkers."

He snapped his fingers. "Bingo. I wouldn't put that sort of thing past her at all. Grayson is still here, and he'll do some of the press with you. But if you would do this, it would be a big help. Can you do it?"

She sighed. "Is the hair and makeup team here for this?"

He nodded. "And wardrobe, too, if you want it."

She looked down at her khakis and ruffled blouse. "Maybe I'll swing by there and pretty up."

"Thanks for doing this, Sierra. I really appreciate it."

"You owe me one for springing this on me, Devon."

"Hey, if I'd told you about the press, would you have come in today?"

"Probably not."

"There you go."

She pursed her lips, but asked, "Where are the reporters going to be set up?"

"On the main soundstage. They'll interview you

on Karen's office set." He glanced at his silver wrist-watch. "They should be arriving within about an hour, so head on over to the prep area and get ready."

"You got it." She stood again and waved as she headed out into the corridor.

An hour and a half later, a perfectly coiffed Sierra sat behind the desk on the set of Karen's office, being interviewed by a woman from a national celebrity news show. The wardrobe stylist had dressed her in one of her character's fine business suits, and Sierra knew that despite her nerves, at least she looked great on camera.

The first interview was followed by three more for television, two for magazines and one for the entertainment column at the *Washington Post*. Grayson was by her side for two television interviews and the one for the newspaper, but she did the rest on her own. When asked the inevitable questions about Mia and her departure from the show, Sierra kept her answers brief, consistent and vague.

"Things weren't working out with Mia on set. We all wish her the best in whatever she decides to do next. I'm not sure what's coming for Fiona, but I'm sure it will be juicy."

By the time the last interviewer left, Sierra dragged herself to her dressing room and flopped down on the love seat. Grabbing a makeup wipe from her purse, she swiped it over her face until it felt clean again, then tossed the wipe in the trash. Exhaustion got the better of her, and before she knew it, she was awakened by someone tapping her on the forehead.

Looking up, she saw Jazmin standing over her. "Girl. Those interviews really took it out of you, didn't they?"

She nodded, sitting upright and stretching. "Yes. How long was I asleep?"

"About an hour. Nobody wanted to wake you, even though you left the door open and we could all hear you snoring."

Embarrassment warmed her cheeks. "Sorry about that."

"No worries. We've all crashed somewhere in the studio after one of those extremely long days. I heard you did seven interviews today."

"I did." She stifled a yawn.

"Then as far as I'm concerned, you earned that nap." She grinned. "Will you be alright driving yourself home, or do you need a ride?"

"I'm good." She stood, getting a full stretch. "Thanks for the offer, though."

"Text me when you get home."

"I will."

Jazmin left, and Sierra shut the door. Changing out of the clothes she'd gotten from wardrobe, she hung them in the dressing room closet and put her own clothes back on. Dressed, she grabbed her purse from the floor. Fishing out the keys to her rental, she left the studio, saying her goodbyes to the folks she passed on the way.

It was after nine now, and full dark had fallen

outside. The half-moon sat high in the sky, partially obscured by a cluster of puffy clouds.

She checked her messages as she got into the car. There was a text from Roland, saying he'd be late for his shift, but nothing else. Shrugging it off, she slipped her phone into the hip pocket of her pants and drove to the condo.

Parking her car, she got out and carried her purse up the stairs. While walking, she thought she heard a sound. Stopping on the top step, she looked around. She had no idea what the sound was, where it had come from or if she'd even actually heard anything. She stood there for a few more moments, scanning the area. When she didn't see anything, she continued to her door.

On the landing, she strolled to the door and stuck her key into the lock.

A moment later, she heard another sound.

She turned, but before she had time to react, someone grabbed her. A strong arm came over her head, clamping her against the body of her unknown assailant. She screamed, struggling to get free.

With his free hand, he raised a blade to her throat.

"Shut up, or I'll slit your throat." His voice was as calm as if he'd asked her the time.

Terrified, she went still and silent.

"Good. Now drop the purse."

She released her grip on the strap, and it fell to the cement floor of the landing.

When he bent to retrieve it, she elbowed him.

He swung out with the knife, and a stripe of red-hot pain seared her arm.

She ignored it, reaching out to twist the doorknob.

Slamming the door before the man could follow her inside, she leaned her back against it, panting and gasping for air.

She could hear his angry shouts from the other side. The door shook as he pummeled it.

Reaching to her left, she flipped open the plastic cover and smashed the red panic button on the alarm panel. The high-pitched wail of the system's sirens rang all around her.

The pounding stopped, and she assumed he'd run away, though she didn't dare look.

She looked at her arm, saw the slashed sleeve and the bright red blood staining it.

Sliding down the door, she sat on the floor and dissolved into tears.

The moment Campbell pulled onto the street leading to The Glenn, he heard the sirens. He'd been headed over to see Sierra, to talk to her about what had happened in New York, and in the days since. He sped up, pushing the speed limit to make it to the complex. When he got there, the guard let him in and he drove to Sierra's unit as fast as he could without the strategically placed speed bumps destroying his undercarriage.

He parked next to her car and got out, sprinting up the stairs.

He pounded on her closed door, calling her name. "Sierra! Sierra, it's Campbell. Are you in there?"

She opened the door, and his heart sank. Her eyes were red and swollen, her face still wet with tears. Aside from that, the left arm of her blouse had been slashed, and the fabric was stained with blood.

Seeing her hurt this way made him seethe with rage. He opened his arms, and she fell into them. "What happened?"

"I was robbed. A man with a knife took my purse and…" She couldn't say more as she began sobbing.

He rubbed her back. "It's okay. I'm here." He looked around then, realizing something was very off. "The real question is, where the hell is your security guard?"

"Roland wasn't here. He texted me…said he would be late."

Campbell shook his head. "Well, this is a fine kettle of fish."

Two police cars pulled up, and Sheriff Jarrod Riordan himself climbed out of one of them. While he climbed the stairs, he called out, "What the hell's going on up there, Cam?"

He gestured for Jarrod to come up. "She's been robbed."

"Holy smokes." Jarrod picked up the pace. When he saw her arm, he called down to the officer getting out of the second car, "Get an ambulance over here."

The next couple hours passed in a whirlwind of activity. The paramedics came, and while Sierra didn't need to be transported, they did clean her wound and patch up her arm with liquid stitches. Jarrod and his deputy took her statements, taking notes on everything she remembered about her ordeal. When Roland finally showed up for his shift, he received a stern reprimand from Jarrod, who threatened to bust him down to station janitor if he didn't straighten up.

After the police cleared out and Roland took up his post on the landing, Campbell took Sierra to the bedroom. He helped her change into a nightgown, careful not to touch or stretch her wound. When she was changed, he tucked her into the bed and sat down on the edge of it.

Her eyes were still damp when she lay down. "Campbell, stay with me. Please."

"You know Roland is right outside your door."

"I know. But I need you to stay in here with me." She grabbed his hand. "I don't want to be alone."

How could she say she needs me, when she's never told me how she feels? He sighed, nodded. "Sure, I'll stay. Now you just try to get some rest, okay?"

She closed her eyes.

As he sat and watched her, Campbell wondered what to do next. Inwardly, he kicked himself for letting his feelings for her develop into something this serious. He'd opened his heart to her, and she'd offered nothing concrete in return.

When he'd left his house to come here, he'd had every intention of telling her he didn't think they should see each other anymore. He'd left her to sleep alone in the bed in New York, and she hadn't protested. Nor had she offered much in the way of conversation on the return flight. Now, after what she'd gone through, he couldn't think of any good way to tell her that. Leaving her alone in this fragile state seemed wrong, even though he didn't want to get more deeply involved with her right now.

The part of him that had already fallen in love with her was at war with the logical part of him that knew this could never work. But what could he do? If he left her now, he'd be the biggest heel in all existence.

He lay across the foot of her bed and stared at the ceiling, much the same way he had that night in New York. Only this time, they were back on his home turf, and he was still just as confused about where all this would lead.

He didn't realize he'd fallen asleep until he woke up to find her gently shaking him.

"Campbell. Hold me?" she whispered to him in the darkness.

Obliging her, he moved to the top of the bed. Taking off his shoes, he slipped under the covers with her, fully clothed, and took her into his arms.

She sighed as she snuggled close to him, and before long, sleep claimed her.

He lay in the dark for a long time, listening to her measured breaths in the silence.

Chapter 16

"Here's your green tea, Sierra."

"Thanks, Jazzy." Sierra grasped the steaming mug by the handle and set it on the coffee table to cool.

Jazmin sat down on the other end of sofa, with her own cup in hand. "I'm glad I came over. You look like hell, girl."

"It's been a rough few days." It was Wednesday, two days since her ordeal, and she still felt uneasy about leaving the condo.

Blowing some of the steam away from her cup, Jazmin took a tentative sip. She wrinkled her nose. "Ugh. Needs some lemon."

"There are some in the produce bin in the fridge."

As Jazmin went to the kitchen, Sierra sighed and

sank deeper into the sofa cushions. Her whole world had been turned upside down, and she couldn't figure out how to cope with it. She knew she'd have to leave the condo eventually, but she didn't know when she'd have the strength. She wouldn't characterize what she felt as fear; it was more like exhaustion, and a general sense of unease. *I just don't have the energy to be around people right now.*

Jazmin returned then and dropped a slice of lemon into her teacup before sitting down again. "Let's talk about it, Sierra. Tell me what happened."

She recapped the assault, and the aftermath, for her friend. "The police chief called me, said they already arrested the man who robbed me. The security footage showed him crawling through the gate behind a car, out of the guard's line of vision. Then he got onto the landing using a grappling hook." She threw up her hands. "A freaking grappling hook. Can you believe it?"

Jazmin's eyes widened. "That guy was on some type of adventure movie kick. It seems a little much for a small-time purse-snatching."

She shook her head. "It is. There's more to it, and I hope the police are grilling his ass real good to find out all the details."

"Well, what happened with Campbell? You said he got here before the police."

"He did. Apparently, he was already on the way here and heard the panic alarm going off." She yawned. "He stayed with me that night. Yesterday morning when I woke up, Campbell was getting ready to leave. I wanted him to stay, but he had to go back to work."

"You don't want the man losing his job, do you?"

"It's a family business. He's not going to lose his job." She frowned. "But that's not the biggest issue."

"Then tell me what is." Jazmin sat back against the cushions with her cup.

"He was just so standoffish with me. I mean, he stayed with me that night, but didn't seem like he wanted to be here. He barely said two words to me the next morning before he rushed out the door." She ran her hand over her scarf-wrapped hair. "I don't know what's going on with him." He'd held her while she slept, like she'd asked. Still, his embrace had been different. It lacked the warmth she was used to getting from him.

"Have you asked him?"

"There wasn't time to." She reached for her mug, sipping the tea and letting the sweet warmth of it wash down her throat. "I was exhausted that night, and he was in such a hurry to leave in the morning."

Jazmin shook her head. "I'm sorry you're going through all this, girl. But try to give Campbell the benefit of the doubt."

She twisted her mouth to the side. "Why should I?"

"He's a good guy, but he's still a guy. Odds are he had no clue what you were feeling."

"I felt vulnerable and uneasy."

"You never told him that. You said so yourself." Jazmin set her tea down on the table. "Remember, men don't think the way we do. If you don't explicitly tell them something, they aren't going to know."

She sighed. "Maybe so. But after what I went through, you would think he could muster a little more sympathy." She'd come to care about Campbell since they'd started spending time together, and based on what he'd said before, he was in love with her. He'd been so closed off since New York, and she couldn't really blame him. *How am I going to get myself out of the mess I've made between us?*

"That's another thing about guys. They can be pretty short on emotional support sometimes." Jazmin patted Sierra's leg. "Luckily, that's what friends are for. As long as you got your girl squad, you'll be good."

"You know, I was starting to think Campbell was different from all the other men I've dated." She folded her arms over her chest, feeling her frustration rise. "But it turns out he's just like the rest."

"How so?"

"These men have bought into the stereotype that the media keeps pushing about me. No matter what I do or where I go, people will always see me as an ice queen." She'd pretty much played the part in her interactions with Campbell over the weekend, and knowing that only made her feel guiltier.

"That's not true. I don't see you that way, Sierra."

"I know. But every man I've been with seems to

believe it. You know what they say. If you keep repeating a lie, eventually people will think it's true."

Jazmin's expression changed, conveying sadness. "Oh, Sierra."

"Men just can't see me as a flesh and blood woman, with real feelings and real vulnerability." She felt the tears sting her eyes. "And Campbell is no exception."

Jazmin scooted close and held out her arms, and Sierra let herself be enfolded.

When Jazmin released her, she gently gripped Sierra's shoulders and looked into her eyes. "Listen, girl. You can't just be laid up in here crying like this. If you want to know where you stand with Campbell, go talk to him."

She sighed. "I don't have a good feeling about this, Jazzy."

"I get that. But either way, it's better to just hash it out with him. Find out what the deal is so you can move forward."

She'd been friends with Jazmin for years and had never known her to give bad advice. Snatching a tissue from the box on the table, she swiped it over her face to dry her tears. "You're right. I need to settle things with him."

Campbell looked over the piles of paperwork scattered over his desk and groaned. Just a few days ago, he'd finally caught up on this stuff, or at least he thought he had. That was before that fated staff meeting, where Savion had announced his plans to input all the old records from their parents' tenure into the computer system. Now he had to comb through stacks of handwritten carbon copies from the eighties and render them digitally. His interns were both working on the same project, but the task was so large, he had no choice but to join in.

He glanced at the clock on his office wall, and saw that it was almost 6:00 p.m. He'd been at his desk for four straight hours, but he wanted to try and tie up one last folder before he headed home for the day.

There was only one good thing that came of doing all this work. It provided a convenient distraction from thinking about Sierra. She hadn't reached out to him at all since he'd left her condo the day before, and he was partly relieved. He didn't know what to say to her, anyway.

He'd left there in a hurry, eager to escape her clinging to him. She'd spent the whole night wrapped around him like moss on a tree, and generally he would have enjoyed that. But since he'd revealed his feelings to her, and she still hadn't said anything about her own feelings, he didn't feel comfortable with her anymore. At least, not at the level he had before. Was she playing some kind of game with him? Was she testing him, to see how much she could get out of him, now that she knew he loved her?

He pushed the thoughts away for what seemed like the millionth time and set to work on the contents of the folder. His hands flew over the keys as he inputted the data from the forms into the matching form on the screen.

He heard a knock at his door and glanced up from his computer screen. Surprise hit him when he saw her standing in the doorway. "Sierra. What are you doing here?"

"We need to talk, Campbell." She appeared somewhat nervous as she brushed her palms over the thighs of her dark denim jeans. "Do you mind if I come in?"

"Close the door." He gestured to the guest chairs on the opposite side of his desk.

She entered the office, shut the door and sat down.

"So, what do you want to talk about?"

"Us. Campbell, I need to know what's going on between us."

He leaned back in his chair, tenting his fingers. "Can you be more specific?"

She appeared annoyed. "Here's the first question. Why didn't you seriously pursue a security detail for me, back when I initially made my request?"

He didn't care for her tone. "Wait a minute. I told you that I reached out to more than one agency on the mainland about that."

"Yes, and you also told me you never followed up with them." She crossed her legs. "Why not?"

He didn't dare tell her what he was thinking, so he toned it down. "I told you these things take a little time. Plus, Sapphire Shores is one of the safest places in the world. We rarely have any crimes committed here, and when we do, it's usually minor stuff. Petty crime, and mostly committed by people from the mainland."

Her eyes widened. "Is that what you call what happened to me? Petty crime?" Her tone grew incredulous. "Did you know that man, who threatened me with a knife, took my purse and damn near slashed my arm open, used a grappling hook to get on the landing? Does that sound like 'petty crime' to you?"

He shook his head. "No. But you have to understand that what happened to you was an anomaly. It's the exception around here, not the rule. I know the crime rate in LA is out of control, but Sapphire Shores is a whole different kind of place."

"So now you want to disparage my hometown." She folded her arms over her chest. "I grew up in the suburbs, by the way, not South Central."

"Sierra, you're overreacting. I'm sorry about what happened. But Jarrod told me they collared the guy, and he's off the streets."

"That's true. I got my ID back, as well as my wallet. Everything else is gone, though."

"I'm sorry about all that."

"Fine. Since that problem is apparently solved, let's move on. What has been with you lately?"

"What are you talking about?"

"I'm talking about how you've been acting lately. The way you rushed out of the condo yesterday. The way you acted as if you didn't want to be there with me the night I was robbed."

So she noticed it. I guess there is something to that whole "women's intuition" thing. "I haven't changed, Sierra. I've just gotten more cautious."

She frowned. "I don't understand."

"You heard me tell you I loved you that night, Sierra. I know you did."

She felt silent, just as he'd expected.

He shook his head. "You've never brought it up. When we were in New York, you seemed stressed, agitated. And when I tried to offer comfort, you pushed me away."

"Campbell, I didn't—"

He held up his hand. "Save it, Sierra. You're beautiful, and you're a stellar actress. I'm always going to be a fan of your work, but your real life is just too damn dramatic for me."

Tears sprang to her eyes. "How could you say that?"

"Because it's true. All this endless babbling about your problems, and never listening to mine. Leaning on me for support, but never offering anything in return. I just don't have time for this, Sierra. You remind me way too much of Tiffany."

Her eyes widened. "You're comparing me to your ex?"

He said nothing. What more needed to be said?

She stood. When she spoke, her voice trembled. "If that's the way you see me, Campbell, then you don't have to worry about me 'leaning on you' anymore. It's over between us." With the tears running down her face, she turned and walked out of his office, and out of his life.

Chapter 17

Sierra awakened Thursday morning with a pounding headache. Blinking her eyes to adjust to the morning sunlight, she reached up and rubbed her temples in a circular motion, hoping to ease the pain. Massaging helped her headache but did nothing to soothe the ache in her heart.

She rolled out of bed, headed for the bathroom. After she'd taken care of her needs, she trudged barefoot to the kitchen to turn on the coffee machine. She opened the fridge and looked inside for a few minutes before realizing she didn't have an appetite for food. Shutting the door, she brewed and fixed her coffee.

On the sofa with her cup, she grabbed the remote

and turned on the television. She flipped to a twenty-four-hour news station and left it there, even though she had no interest in the headlines. All she wanted was a distraction, something to take her mind off Campbell.

She'd been the one to end things, and at the time, it seemed like the right thing to do. Now she wasn't so sure. *What if he's the one?*

The ringing of her phone dragged her out of her thoughts and into the real world again. She grabbed it from the coffee table and answered it. "Hello?"

"Good morning, Ms. Dandridge. This is Chief Riordan at SSPD."

She sat up. "Good morning."

"I'm calling you to let you know that we've put out a warrant for Mia Leigh's arrest."

Her eyes widened. "What? Why?"

"We've been searching through and archiving your social media posts, just as you requested. While we were doing that, we discovered that Ms. Leigh had shared your location with someone online."

"Oh, no." A cold shiver ran down her spine. "Was it a public post?"

"No. But when we confronted Mr. Holt, the man we arrested for the robbery, he told us that Ms. Leigh shared the information with him via a private message. It took some digging, because Ms. Leigh used a service that deletes messages after a set period. But we found the exchange that corroborated Mr. Holt's story."

She dropped her head in her hands. *I was wrong about Mia. She really didn't deserve all the chances I gave her.* "What's going to happen to Mia now?"

"We need you to come down to the station and talk with our detectives about that. She's been caught, and she needs to pay for what she's done." Jarrod paused. "How she's punished will be left up to you as the injured party, at least partly."

"I understand." She thought of something. "Just one more question."

"Go ahead."

"Any idea why he used a grappling hook?"

Jarrod chuckled. "Sorry, I shouldn't be laughing, but it is somewhat humorous. Turns out he works in the props department at a studio in Wilmington, and just wanted to try it out."

Sierra rolled her eyes. "That's the stupidest thing I've heard all day."

"I agree. And I seriously doubt he has a job to go back to at this point."

She could only shake her head.

"I don't know if it helps to hear this, but he did say he was sorry he cut you. He claims he never meant to hurt you, just to scare you."

"I guess it helps. A little." Unfortunately, Mr. Holt's crisis of conscience wouldn't do anything to heal the cut he'd left on her arm.

"You know we recovered your wallet with your ID, but we still haven't retrieved your purse or any of the other contents."

"That figures." She hadn't been carrying anything particularly valuable, though she did lament the loss of her favorite compact mirror, hairbrush and the few pairs of earrings scattered in the bottom of her bag. The couple hundred dollars in cash she'd had in her wallet would be easily replaced.

"How soon can you come down to the station?"

"In about an hour. Would that work?"

"Sure. See you then." He disconnected the call.

She got up and went to the bedroom. Going to seek justice would provide a welcome distraction from wallowing in her mixed emotions about what had happened between her and Campbell. No matter what, she vowed not to be seen in public looking a mess. So she pulled herself together and donned a pair of bright white jeans, a lavender drop needle sweater and a pair of bejeweled ballet flats. Once she was dressed, she hid her tear-swollen eyes behind a pair of large, dark sunglasses. Grabbing the purse she'd been carrying since her favorite one had been stolen, she armed the alarm system, locked up the condo and left for the police station.

Seated in Jarrod's office at the station, she was shown all the information he and his staff had uncovered. Of all the images and documents she looked at, she was most affected by Mia's mug shot. She appeared as a shell of the woman Sierra had worked with. Her hair was unkempt, her face streaked with tears, and her eyes were wide and fearful.

Sierra covered her mouth with her hands. "Wow.

I've never seen her look that rough. She had a terrible attitude, but she was always well put together."

"Finding out you're going to jail will do that to a person." Jarrod tucked the mug shot and the other documents into an orange envelope and sealed the gold clasp at the top. "I see it all the time. Even the wealthiest, most successful people can be reduced to tears when their bad decisions catch up to them."

"Did she really send that man to attack me?"

He shook his head. "No. The messages we found show that she never asked him to do anything to you. She merely shared your location with him. From what we can tell, Mr. Holt did the rest of his own volition."

"I see."

"Still, what Ms. Leigh did is a class 2 misdemeanor under the North Carolina Cyberstalking Law. She's going to be fined at least a thousand dollars, and she'll have to pay you some kind of restitution, as well."

Even though he'd put everything away, Sierra couldn't get the image of Mia out of her mind. "Chief, will she end up in prison?"

He shook his head. "Call me Jarrod. And no, not for an offense like this."

"Okay, Jarrod. I can tell you right now that I don't want Mia's money."

His thick brow cocked. "Come again?"

"I may be crazy, but I think what Mia needs is

counseling, not punishment. There have to be some underlying issues to explain her irrational behavior."

He shrugged. "That's possible. The arresting officer did tell me she didn't fight, just sobbed all the way to lockup."

Sierra drew a deep breath. "I don't know why I feel sympathy for Mia. Lord knows she's treated me like crap. But is there a way we can arrange for her to get some counseling?"

"You mean, have her committed?"

"Not necessarily. Get her evaluated, and let a psychiatrist decide if that's what she needs."

"So, you're saying you'd like her to get counseling as a way of paying her restitution."

"Yes."

"Sounds reasonable. But that doesn't offer you much protection if she has another lapse in judgment." He tented his fingers, rested his elbows on the desk. "I hear what you're saying about keeping her out of prison. But why don't we add a protective order, saying Ms. Leigh needs to stay away from you?"

She nodded slowly. "I can agree to that. I don't want her in prison, but I don't want her near me, either."

"Great." He pulled out a pad of forms and flipped to a blank one. "Let's set up some standard terms. Ms. Leigh is to have no contact with you, online, in person, by mail or telephone, for at least one year. She is also to keep a physical distance of at least two hundred and fifty yards away from you at all times." He looked to her for approval. "How does that sound?"

"Sounds fair."

He jotted some information on the form. "We'll also leave this open for amendment. If in a year she's not completed her counseling, or there's any other reason to extend the order, we can do it at that time." He finished writing on the form, then slid it to her. "Initial, sign and print your name on those last three lines, please."

She did as he instructed, then slid the pad back to him. "Is there anything else I need to do?"

"No. We'll keep you informed of the process as we move forward. Have a good day, Ms. Dandridge."

"Thank you." Rising from her chair, and feeling confident she'd done the right thing, she exited.

Friday afternoon, Campbell settled into his recliner for his eighth episode of *Bass Masters*. He'd been surfing the channels for something to watch one day when he stumbled upon a marathon, and had been riveted ever since. Dressed in a pair of old sweats, he pulled the lever to raise his feet. Grabbing the bowl of popcorn from the side table, he munched as he watched the show's host do battle with an epic fish.

This was so much nicer than entering those damn forms into the computer. He'd taken two personal days and hadn't been in the office since Wednesday night, when Sierra had shown up and ripped his heart out of his chest.

He frowned, pushing her out of his mind. It was over between them, and while he'd thought himself in love with her, he'd obviously been mistaken. He didn't need her, didn't need anyone. He was fine just like this, with his comfortable clothes, in his comfortable chair, in his comfortable house living a comfortable life.

Pounding on his door startled him, breaking him out of the hypnotic trance brought on by the rolling waves on the television. *Who the hell is that banging on the damn door?* He rarely ever got time to really relax, and he didn't appreciate having his peace interrupted. He lowered his feet, grumbling as he rose from his chair to answer the door. *This had better be good.*

When he yanked open the door, he found his brother standing on his porch. "Savion, what do you want?"

Dressed in his work attire of a dark suit and tie, Savion looked him up and down, his expression disapproving. "I want you to move so I can come in."

He folded his arms over his chest. "I don't want any visitors."

Savion rolled his eyes, pushing past him into the house. "I'm not a visitor. I'm family."

With a deep sigh, Campbell shut the door. "Thanks for the reminder. Now that you've invited yourself inside my house, maybe you can tell me what you want."

Savion stood by the recliner, pointing to the mess of crumpled napkins, empty soda cans and dropped popcorn kernels. "Gave the maid the week off?"

He pushed past his brother and flopped back down in his chair. "Nah. She just does a terrible job." On the heels of his flip remark about his nonexistent maid, Campbell refocused his attention on the television.

Savion inhaled, then crinkled his nose. "Bro, when's the last time you showered?"

He shrugged. "I haven't gone anywhere, so what does it matter?"

He moved to the sofa. "Fair enough, but since you smell like feet and despair, I'm going over here where I'm not downwind of you."

Campbell glared at his brother.

"Don't cut your eyes at me. You're the one who's boycotting bathing."

He folded his arms over his chest but said nothing. What was the point? Savion didn't know or understand the kind of pain he was in.

"You know something? Being the oldest sibling in this family can be a real pain in the butt." He settled back against the cushions. "At work, I have to shoulder most of the responsibility. Then, outside of work, I'm the one who has to play Mr. Fix-it whenever you or Hadley get yourselves into a mess."

"Nobody asked you to come here, Savion."

"*Au contraire, mon frère.* Mom sent me." He grabbed one of the throw pillows on the couch and tossed it in his direction. "No one has heard from you in two days. You haven't been to work. You're burning through your personal days while your interns bust their asses to get the data migration project done."

He scoffed. "They're young. They've got plenty of energy."

Savion shook his head. "I've got instructions from Mom to get you showered, dressed and over to the house for dinner."

He made a show of settling into his chair. "I'm not going anywhere. I don't feel like it."

"Like I said, Mom is expecting you for dinner. I don't know what's going on with you, or why you're acting this way. You may be crazy, but you know better than to test Viola Monroe."

He groaned. His brother was right. If his mother wanted him to come over for dinner, he wasn't going to have any choice but to leave his hovel and show up.

"I heard about what happened to Sierra on the news, but I know there's something else at play here. You wanna talk about it?"

He stared at him. "You wanna hear it?"

Savion shrugged. "Might as well."

He summarized the argument he'd had at his office Wednesday night with Sierra. "You were already gone home for the night when all this happened. So, go ahead and say it, I know you want to."

"Say what?"

"I told you so. You warned me about Sierra, and I didn't listen." And now he would probably spend the rest of his days kicking himself for getting involved with her, for loving her.

His brother's expression softened to something akin to sympathy. "You love her." He stated it as fact instead of asking.

Feeling the tightness in his chest intensify, Campbell nodded.

"I'm not about to clown you for caring about her, Cam. I'm not a garage human." Savion leaned forward, resting his clasped hands on his lap. "I will tell you that you need to get up from that chair, clean up and get your shit together."

"Why? She walked out on me, so what's the point?"

He shook his head. "If you love her, go after her. Duh."

Campbell blew out a breath, hoping to release some of the pressure he felt inside.

Savion stood. "I don't have all day, man. Mom's serving dinner at seven." He raised his wrist and glanced at his watch. "That gives you about thirty minutes to bathe your funky behind, get dressed and get in the damn car. Got it?"

Climbing out of the soft nest of his easy chair, Campbell stood. "Got it."

"Good. Now scram." Savion pointed toward the steps leading to the upper level.

Campbell trudged by his brother, muttering, "Thanks, Savion."

"Yeah, right. You and Hadley are such a mess." He gave him a firm but gentle push toward the stairs.

Chapter 18

Sierra looked around her apartment in the Pacific Palisades area of Los Angeles Sunday morning, and sighed. It felt good to be back home, though she wished she'd left things in better shape before leaving Sapphire Shores.

She'd enjoyed Campbell's company, she could admit that. She'd probably even come to love him. But none of that mattered now. She couldn't be with a man who couldn't see past her image, to see her for who she really was.

After dealing with the situation at the police station, she'd gotten a call from her agent later than evening. The director she'd met with in Manhattan wanted to offer her the role for the romantic comedy they'd discussed. While on the phone, she'd accepted. In order to prepare for her trip to London, where the movie would be filmed, she'd taken a late afternoon flight home yesterday. Jazmin had agreed to return her rental car and hold on to the keys to the condo until the MHI office opened on Monday morning.

Now she was getting ready for her flight to London. She wished she had more time to hang around her place, but duty called. The director wanted to get an early start on filming promos. He also wanted Sierra to spend some time discussing the nuances of the character and the script with the writers. This would be her first role in a film like this, and she really wanted to nail it. *This is my chance to break out of the ice queen stereotype, in a big way.*

Standing in her bedroom, she looked at the two open suitcases laid out on her bed. She'd packed most of her essentials already, toiletries, makeup and accessories. Now she needed to decide what clothing to take, and how much of it. She'd be in London for several weeks at least, depending on how smoothly the filming progressed.

Her mother entered the room then, with the same disappointed look on her face she'd been wearing all day. Rachel Myers Dandridge, petite and thin, wore a red T-shirt and a pair of khaki shorts. "I wish you didn't have to rush off like this. You just got home, and we hardly get to see you these days."

Sierra smiled, kissed her mother on the forehead. "Mommy, I really need your help packing. I didn't expect you to spend the whole day making me feel guilty about leaving."

"I'm sorry, Sugar Plum. It's just that we miss you." She hugged her around the waist.

Sierra returned her hug. "I know. I miss you and Daddy, too." She tossed a black pencil skirt over her mother's shoulder and into the bag. "Tell you what. Why don't we go pick Daddy up, and the three of us can have brunch?"

Rachel smiled. "That sounds wonderful."

Sierra took her parents out for brunch, then delivered them to their house in Rustic Canyon before returning to her apartment to finish packing. She'd just zipped the first overstuffed suitcase when she heard someone knocking at her door.

Frowning, she walked through the apartment and went to see who it was.

She wasn't expecting visitors and couldn't say she was in the entertaining mood. But she drew a deep breath, bracing for whoever might be on the other side of her door as she looked out the peephole.

Campbell stood, nervously tapping his foot, waiting. The bouquet of two dozen white roses suddenly seemed to weigh a ton.

Finally, Sierra swung open the door, and stared at him, wide-eyed. "Campbell?"

He smiled. "Hi, Sierra."

She looked beautiful in the lavender sundress that just grazed her knees, though her face registered a mixture of shock and confusion. "What are you doing here? And how did you know where I was?"

"I worried the hell out of Jazmin and Devon to find out." He extended the bouquet toward her. "These are for you."

She took them, holding them close to her chest. "They're beautiful. Thank you."

"Would you mind if I came in?"

She stepped aside so he could enter.

"Nice place." He looked around at her domain. She had all white leather furniture and glass-topped stainless steel tables. The walls were painted a soft aqua blue, and she was apparently a collector of African art. Various wooden masks, statuettes and other artifacts decorated the space.

"Thank you." He watched her walk away. He heard water running, then she returned without the flowers. "I put them in water."

"It's funny. I had a speech planned." He clasped his hands together in front of him. "I was repeating it to myself the whole cab ride here from the airport. Now I just want to say what's in my heart."

Her eyes welled with tears. "I'm sorry, Campbell."

He went to her, circling his arms around her waist. "No, no, Sierra. I'm sorry. I shouldn't have acted the way I did. I should have been there for you, without expecting anything in return."

"No." She shook her head. "Relationships are about being there for each other. I should have been more willing to listen to you." She reached up, stroked her palm over his jaw.

Feeling her touch again made his heart thump like the bass line of a pop song. "I love you, Sierra. I'm sorry if I ever made you feel otherwise."

The tears spilled over, running down her cheeks. "I love you, Campbell. Being without you these last few days helped me realize it."

He smiled, then leaned down to kiss her with all the passion he felt inside. When he broke the kiss, he squeezed her hand. "Marry me, Sierra. I don't want to waste another minute."

She gasped. "Are you serious?"

He nodded. "Very."

"Of course I'll marry you." She paused. "Oh, but we can't do it just yet."

"Why not?"

"Remember the meeting in Manhattan? I got the role in that rom-com."

He gave her a squeeze. "That's great! I knew you'd get it. Congratulations!"

"Thanks, Cam. But…"

He noticed the change in her tone. "But what?"

"The movie is filming in England. I'm flying out tomorrow for London, and it will be at least six weeks before I get back to the States."

He thought for a moment. There had to be a solution here. After everything he'd gone through to come here and make amends, he wasn't about to let anything stand in the way of their new life together. He snapped his fingers. "I'll go with you."

Her eyes went wide. "Really? Are you sure you can manage that?"

"Yes, it will be fine. My interns are almost finished with the data migration project. Hadley can oversee the rest of it, until I get back."

"You're really willing to leave your work to someone else, for that long?"

He nodded. "For you? Hell yes. If they really need me, I can always do some telework. I brought my laptop."

She blinked several times, as if still in disbelief. "So, you're going to leave your entire life on the island behind, and fly to London with me, on less than twenty-four hours' notice, and for an unknown amount of time?"

"Yes."

"Wow. I'm so happy, but I'm finding all this hard to believe."

"Trust me, I get it." He pulled her into his embrace. "Baby, if someone had told me a year ago that I'd be in love with you, and ready to drop everything to be with you, I wouldn't have believed it, either. And yet here we are."

She blessed him with that beautiful smile. "Oh, Campbell."

Moments later, he pressed his lips to hers, and kissed her as if both their lives depended on it.

Chapter 19

Five Weeks Later

Sierra stood in the observation pod of the London Eye, with the whole city spread out below. Dressed in a knee-grazing, sequined white cocktail dress, white flats and a feathered white fascinator, she breathed in the happiness of this moment. Campbell looked dashing in a crisp white shirt, tan slacks, brown leather loafers and an authentic brown bowler. The view through the glass was breathtaking, but as she took Campbell's hands in her own and said her wedding vows, she had eyes only for him. They sealed their promise with a kiss, and when their lips met, she was literally and figuratively on top of the world.

After the ceremony, Sierra and Campbell headed to a nearby pub to meet the cast of *Her London Love*, the film she'd just wrapped. When her castmates and the crew had discovered her upcoming nuptials, they'd insisted on celebrating the couple at the cast wrap party. They spent the better part of the evening dancing, drinking and enjoying the company of the people who had become their friends over the last several weeks.

That night, they eschewed staying at their rented flat in favor of spending their wedding night at the swanky Mandarin Oriental Hyde Park Hotel. Inside the well-appointed suite, Sierra relished being alone with her new husband for the first time.

"I love you so much, baby." She kissed him on the lips, then sat on the edge of the bed.

He knelt in front of her, slipping her feet out of her shoes and setting them aside. "I love you, too, Sierra." He began massaging her feet, and she purred.

"Oh, that feels good."

"I figured you'd be sore from all that dancing." He laughed. "Speaking of which, you know my parents will want to throw a party or something when we get back. They love playing hosts."

She sighed. "My parents aren't going to be too happy about us eloping. But I think they'll come around once they see how in love we are."

"I'll be sure to put on a good show for them, then." He winked. "With you, it will be easy to wear my heart on my sleeve."

"Mmm-hmm." She lay back across the bed, tugging up the hem of her dress to reveal the white thong beneath. "That's fine, but let's talk about it later."

He whistled, eyes glowing with desire. "Yes, ma'am. I can see the real party is about to happen right here, right now."

And as his large hand slid up her thigh and slipped between her legs, she closed her eyes and let him take her to paradise.

Epilogue

Late October

Sierra swirled around the dance floor in Campbell's arms, feeling the smile stretch her lips. She could not remember a time when she'd felt so happy, so carefree. The flat shoes she'd chosen helped her maintain her stability as her husband guided her around the floor, and she enjoyed every moment of the dance. When the song ended, the newlyweds weaved through the cheering crowd of guests, back to the head table to sit down.

From her seat, Sierra surveyed the scene. Just as Campbell predicted, his parents had insisted on throwing a reception for them, and she could see that

Viola Monroe had gone all out to plan a wonderful celebration. The big tent, set up on the lawn of the Monroe family estate, bustled with the conversation and activity of the one hundred or more invited guests. White-clothed tables, each topped with fine china, silver and flickering candles, surrounded the glistening dance floor they'd just left.

"Enjoying the party?" Campbell picked up her hand, bringing it to his lips for a kiss.

"Yes. It's been so great meeting so many members of your family." She squeezed his hand. "Do you think they like me?"

He chuckled. "I'm sure of it. Everyone who's met you today loves you, just like I do."

His words warmed her heart, and she smiled. "Glad to hear it."

He fell silent for a moment, taking a sip from his champagne flute. "This may not be the best time to ask, but I have to know. Where do you want to live, now that we're married?"

She could sense him bracing, as if he expected an answer he wouldn't like. "Here."

"Really?" Surprise registered on his face.

She nodded. "When I first came here, I thought the island was so boring compared to LA." She paused, looking into his eyes. "But with you, I have all the excitement I need."

His broad grin gave away his approval. "Great. And if you want to move into a bigger place, we can start building—"

She shook her head. "I don't need that, at least not for now. Maybe after the babies come along."

He leaned in to kiss her cheek. "Babies, eh?"

"You know it. But for right now, all I need is you." She released a contented sigh.

Hadley walked by then, tapping her on the shoulder as she passed. "There's a show going on, Sierra. Five o'clock." She pointed, and continued walking past the table.

Sierra turned, looking where Hadley had indicated. Eyes widening, she poked Campbell in the forearm. "Holy cow, Cam. Look."

He shifted his gaze, as well. "Well, damn."

There, just left of the center of the dance floor, were Savion and Jazmin. Their bodies pressed close together, they swayed to the strains of L.T.D.'s classic soul hit "Love Ballad." Savion whispered something to Jazmin, and she giggled.

Sierra and Campbell watched the scene unfold before them. When they turned to look at each other again, they both laughed.

She shook her head in amazement. "Think anything will come of it?"

He shrugged. "Who knows? But if it does, I'm definitely going to tease him about it."

She smiled, wagged her index finger near his face. "Oh, no, you won't. You'll be too busy entertaining your new bride." She left her chair, easing onto his lap and folding her arms around his neck.

He groaned low in his throat as he pulled her

close. "True. And I plan to keep you so warm, your new nickname will be Fire Bird."

She felt the shiver of anticipation run through her body. "I love you, Campbell."

"Not half as much as I love you, Sierra." And he drew her in for a long, sweet kiss.

* * * * *

KIMANI™ ROMANCE

COMING NEXT MONTH
Available September 18, 2018

#589 SEDUCTIVE MEMORY
Moonlight and Passion • by AlTonya Washington
A chance encounter with Paula Starker is all entrepreneur Linus Brooks needs to try to win back the sultry Philadelphia DA. And where better to romance her than on a tropical island? But before they can share a future, Linus will have to reveal his tragic secret...

#590 A LOS ANGELES PASSION
Millionaire Moguls • by Sherelle Green
Award-winning screenwriter Trey Moore agrees to look after his infant nephew for two weeks. Gorgeous Kiara Woods, owner of LA's glitziest day care, offers to help. While she's teaching Trey babysitting 101, she's falling hard for the millionaire. But can she risk revealing a painful truth that's already cost her so much?

#591 HER PERFECT PLEASURE
Miami Strong • by Lindsay Evans
Lawyer and businessman Carter Diallo solves problems for his powerful family's corporation. But when his influential powers fail him, the Diallos bring in PR wizard—and Carter's ex-lover—Jade Tremaine. Ten years ago, Carter left Jade emotionally devastated. Now the guy known as The Magic Man must win back Jade's trust...

#592 TEMPTING THE BILLIONAIRE
Passion Grove • by Niobia Bryant
Betrayed by his fiancée, self-made billionaire Chance Castillo plans to sue his ex for her share of their million-dollar wedding. His unexpected attraction to his new attorney takes his mind off his troubles. But Ngozi Johns *never* dates a client. Until one steamy night with the gorgeous Dominican changes *everything*.

KPCNM0918

Get 4 FREE REWARDS!

We'll send you 2 FREE Books plus 2 FREE Mystery Gifts.

Harlequin® Desire books feature heroes who have it all: wealth, status, incredible good looks... everything but the right woman.

FREE Value Over **$20**

"I had a nice time tonight," Kiara said when she reached the door. When she didn't hear a response, she turned around to find him watching her intently.

"I had a nice time, as well." Trey took a step closer to her. "I enjoyed getting to know you a little better." He was so close, Kiara was afraid to breathe.

"Me, too," she whispered. His eyes dropped to her lips and stayed there for a while. After a few moments, she forced herself to swallow the lump in her throat.

He took another step closer, so she took another step back, only to be met with the door. When his hand reached up to cup her face, Kiara completely froze. *There's no way he's going to kiss me, right? We just met each other.*

"Do you want me to stop?" he asked.

Say yes. Say yes. Say yes. "No," she said, moments before his lips came crashing down onto hers. Her hands flew to the back of his neck as he gently pushed her against the door. Kiara had experienced plenty of first kisses in the past, but this was unlike any first kiss she'd ever had. Trey's lips were soft, yet demanding. Eager, yet controlled. When she parted her lips to get a better taste, his tongue briefly swooped into her mouth before he ended their kiss with a soft peck and backed away.

Kiara couldn't be sure how she looked, but she certainly felt unhinged and downright aroused.

"Come on," Trey said with a nod. "I'll walk you to your car."

How is he even functioning after that kiss? Kiara felt like she glided to the car, rather than walked. Yet Trey looked as composed as ever.

"We should get together again soon," Trey said, opening her car door. Kiara sat down in the driver's seat and looked up at Trey. He flashed her a sexy smile.

"And for the record, this was definitely a date," Trey said with a wink. "I didn't stop kissing you because I wasn't enjoying it, nor was I trying to tease you. I stopped kissing you because if I hadn't, I'd be ready to drag you into my bedroom. Which also brings me to the reason I didn't show you my bedroom. I didn't trust myself not to make a move." Trey leaned a little closer. "When we make love, I want us to know one another a little better, so I forced myself to stop kissing you tonight and it was damn hard to do so. Have a good night, Kiara."

Trey softly kissed her cheek and closed her door before she could vocalize a response. Quite frankly, she didn't think she had anything to say anyway. Her mind was still reeling and her lips were still tingling from that explosive kiss.

Kiara gave a quick wave. *I told you not to get out of the car earlier*, that voice in her head teased. She started her car and drove away from Trey's house.

"What the hell just happened?" She'd originally thought that she could avoid him or keep their relationship strictly friendly. Now she wasn't so sure. Kissing Trey had awakened desires she thought she'd long buried. Feelings she'd ignored and pushed aside.

Kiara made it to her home a few minutes later. She glanced at her house before dropping her head to the steering wheel. She was in deep and she knew it. To make matters worse, she only lived a five-minute drive from Trey's house, meaning there was no way she was getting any sleep tonight knowing a man that sexy was only a couple miles away.

Don't miss A Los Angeles Passion
*by Sherelle Green, available October 2018
wherever Harlequin® Kimani Romance™
books and ebooks are sold.*

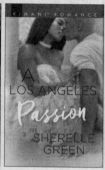